You're invited to a

CREEPOVER™

RL AUG 2014

There's Something Out There

written by P. J. Night

SIMON SPOTLIGHT

New York   London   Toronto   Sydney   New Delhi

This book is a work of fiction. Any references to historical events, real people, or real locales are used fictitiously. Other names, characters, places, and incidents are the product of the author's imagination, and any resemblance to actual events or locales or persons, living or dead, is entirely coincidental.

SIMON SPOTLIGHT
An imprint of Simon & Schuster Children's Publishing Division
1230 Avenue of the Americas, New York, New York 10020
Copyright © 2011 by Simon & Schuster, Inc.
All rights reserved, including the right of reproduction in whole or in part in any form.
SIMON SPOTLIGHT and colophon are registered trademarks of Simon & Schuster, Inc.
YOU'RE INVITED TO A CREEPOVER is a trademark of Simon & Schuster, Inc.
Text by Ellie O'Ryan
Designed by Nicholas Sciacca
For information about special discounts for bulk purchases, please contact Simon & Schuster Special Sales at 1-866-506-1949 or business@simonandschuster.com.
Manufactured in the United States of America 0413 OFF
First Edition 10 9 8 7 6 5 4
Library of Congress Cataloging-in-Publication Data
Night, P. J. There's something out there / by P.J. Night. — 1st ed. p. cm. — (You're invited to a creepover) Summary: On a sleepover at her house, Jenna and her friends go in search of the legendary Marked Monster that is said to roam the forests around her hometown. [1. Sleepovers—Fiction. 2. Monsters—Fiction. 3. Horror stories.] I. Title. PZ7.N576Th 2012
[Fic]—dc23 2011024190 ISBN 978-1-4424-4148-4 ISBN 978-1-4424-4149-1 (eBook)

CHAPTER 1

What happened in the woods that night changed every-thing, forever, and if the girl had known what was going to happen, she never would have left her house.

But she didn't know, see? She didn't have a clue what was waiting for her, so when she heard the scratching, she thought it was the stray cat that had been coming around. The one with the tattered ear and the hungry eyes.

The sun was just about to set. She could see it still shining in the west, like an orange ball of fire on the verge of falling into space. *So,* she thought, *I'll just put some food at the edge of the yard. For the cat.*

She poured a cup of kitty chow into a plastic bag and grabbed her coat. Then she walked out the back door, into the dying light, like it was no big deal, because it wasn't . . . not yet.

At the edge of the yard, she looked for the cat by the tree stump where it usually waited for her. The cat's fur was so black that at night, all you could see was its eyes gleaming in the darkness. But tonight, the cat was nowhere to be seen.

"Here, kitty, kitty," she called softly, kneeling down and snapping her fingers like she always did.

Still the cat did not appear.

The girl sighed. The air was damp, as if the fog were rushing in faster tonight than usual, hardly waiting for the sun to finish setting before blanketing the woods in a thick mist that was impossible to see through. She felt so sorry for the poor cat, sleeping in the woods all alone, even when it was cold or windy or wet.

Then she heard it again: the scratching. Just beyond the tree line. And—what was that? A whimper?

The girl glanced behind her at the house, still all lit up, so warm and cozy. She wanted to go back there.

So why was she walking toward the woods?

Because she couldn't bear it, the thought that the cat was sick or hurt, or in trouble.

If she could help the little cat, she would.

"Here, kitty," she called again, pushing through the tree limbs. "I won't hurt you. Here, kitty."

Silence.

That the woods should be so chillingly quiet, the girl realized, was weird. Very weird. But instead of feeling afraid, she was curious.

She should have been afraid.

On she continued into the woods, all the way to the clearing where she'd spent so many summer nights on campouts, telling stories in the flickering light of a campfire. She knew that clearing as well as she knew her own bedroom, but she'd never seen it the way she did tonight.

It was hard to see through the mist, but she could tell right away that the clearing was not empty.

And whatever was in it was a *lot* bigger than a stray cat.

The girl hid behind a thick-trunked tree, her heart thundering in her chest, and stared with wide eyes. She couldn't have looked away even if she'd wanted to.

Well, to be honest, she did want to look away. But her eyes were locked on the creature, and she wondered, suddenly, if she was dreaming.

But she knew that that was nothing more than a

wish, an empty hope. Because nothing had ever felt this real—from the painful pounding of her heart to the bitter taste of fear in the back of her throat.

The monster was eating . . . something. Dark red liquid dripped from its mouth, soaking into the dirt beneath it. The girl's stomach lurched, but still she did not move.

Then, to her horror, the creature reared up on its hind legs at the same moment the mist cleared. In the dim twilight, she saw more of it than she ever wanted to: an enormous lizardlike body, covered in scales and slime.

Two tremendous, leathery wings, folded tight against its back.

Two thick, stumpy arms; the end of each one curved with razor-sharp talons, dripping . . . something. Something foul.

Back legs that rippled with muscle.

A knobby, bumpy head, with two red-rimmed, beady eyes, and a mouthful of fangs.

And a tail that was studded with spikes as long as the girl's forearm.

Perhaps the worst, though, the memory she would never forget: Along its waxy underbelly ran an angry, raised scar that was barely visible in the fading light. It was obviously an old injury; she could tell from the way the skin puckered around it. Yet still it oozed as if it would never heal.

The creature was like nothing she had ever seen before: part bird, part lizard.

All monster.

It tilted its head to the side, rotating slowly . . . slowly . . . until—no, it couldn't be—wait—it was— it was *staring right at her*, the pupil of that horrible eye dilating as it focused on what it wanted.

Then, more powerfully than she ever could have imagined, the creature leaped through the clearing, directly to the tree she was hiding behind. One of its talons sliced through the darkness but somehow missed her, and got stuck in the thick tree trunk instead of in the girl's skull.

Suddenly she was no longer rooted to the ground in terror; she was running for her life, crashing through the underbrush back to the safety of her house. The creature struggled to get free, screaming in frustration as it watched its prey escape. And it sounded like—

It sounded like—

CHAPTER 2

"Aiiiii-ck-ck-ck-ck!" Jenna Walker shrieked, so shrilly and bone-chillingly that all the other girls cried out in horror and clapped their hands over their ears. A satisfied smile flickered across Jenna's face. Her story was definitely the scariest one by far, and she hadn't even gotten to the really freaky part yet.

"Somehow, thanks to the trunk of that old pine tree, the girl made it back to her house," Jenna continued in a slow, quiet voice that made everyone else go completely silent. "She waited all night for the creature to follow her there, to smash through the windows. But it never did.

"And the next day, in the bright morning sun, she dared to step outside again. The woods were full of sound: chattering squirrels, chirping birds, scurrying chipmunks. The girl used the sounds to gauge the danger and decided that if the woodland creatures felt safe enough to be out, she should feel safe too. So, one step at a time, she returned to the clearing."

Jenna paused. She took a deep breath and looked at each one of her friends for a moment before she continued.

"There was no sign of the creature. No sign of whatever it had been eating, or the blood that had soaked into the ground. There weren't even any tracks. The girl started to feel embarrassed. Foolish. Had she imagined it? Was it all a dream? And then . . . she saw . . . this."

Jenna reached behind her back and, in one fast move, whipped her arm around, her hand held high. The enormous talon gleamed in the beam from the flashlights. Once more, everyone screamed, just as she'd known they would.

"Stuck in the tree . . . the claw of the Marked Monster!" she announced.

"*Ewww!* What is that?" Brittany shrieked.

"Jenna, wow. That was the scariest story, no doubt," Jenna's best friend, Maggie, said, shivering. "I'm not going to sleep at all tonight."

"True," Laurel chimed in. "Way to go, Jenna. You totally win that round."

Jenna grinned at her friends. For the last three years, they'd been having sleepovers at least twice a month, and this was always her favorite part: telling scary stories. After the girls had eaten pizza and popcorn, after they'd watched movies and given each other pedicures, after everyone else in the house was asleep, they turned out all the lights, lit up their flashlights, and tried to freak each other out. Sometimes Jenna spent the entire week before a slumber party trying to think up a scary story to top the last one she'd told, spending hours searching for creepy tales on the Internet. That's where she had learned all about the Marked Monster. Jenna had even read a description of its haunting shriek.

Brittany's face wrinkled up in disgust as she stared at the claw. "That is too gross. Where did you get it?"

"What do you mean, where did I get?" Jenna replied. "I just told you. I pulled it out of the pine tree in the clearing behind my house."

"Wait—that was *you*?" Brittany asked. "*You* are the girl in that story?"

"Well, duh," Jenna said. "Really? You guys didn't get

that? We've only camped out in that clearing, like, a hundred times."

Brittany shook her head. "No way. That story is not true. You probably just got the claw at the Halloween store or something."

"You wish I did," Jenna shot back. "I mean, yeah, I didn't see the Marked Monster in the woods or anything—that part I made up. But I did find its claw in the tree. Trust me, the claw is the real deal. Here. See for yourself."

She leaned forward and dropped the claw in Brittany's lap. Brittany jumped up so fast that the claw clattered across the floor. "Get that nasty bird toenail away from me! It's probably covered in germs!"

Everyone cracked up then, and Brittany's face got all red. "You think it's so funny?" she asked, but when she started laughing, the other girls knew she wasn't really mad. "Here you go. Why don't you spend some quality time with it?"

She scooped the claw off the floor and tossed it toward Maggie, who shrieked as she caught it and immediately chucked it toward Laurel.

"Ack! Get it away! I don't want it!" Laurel cried, throwing it wildly toward Jenna.

Too wildly.

There was no way for Jenna to catch the talon as it soared toward her; there wasn't even enough time for her to move out of the way. She heard the rip of her sleeve; she felt the burn as the talon sliced through her skin; and they all heard the *thunk* as the talon smacked against the wall behind her and plunged to the floor.

Jenna sucked in her breath sharply and grabbed her arm. She felt something hot and wet soaking through her torn sleeve.

"Oh no, no, no, are you okay?" Laurel asked in a rush. "Oh, Jenna, I'm so sorry, I didn't mean—"

"No, it's cool. It was just an accident," Jenna said, biting the inside of her cheek as she tried not to cry. She didn't want to be a big baby about it. It was just a little cut.

But it really, really hurt.

Maggie and Brittany leaped into action.

"I'll get a clean T-shirt for you to wear," Maggie said.

"Mags, where's your first-aid kit?" Brittany asked. "Or some Band-Aids or something?"

"Come with me; I'll show you," Maggie said, and the two girls hurried out of the room.

"What can I do?" Laurel asked, hovering around Jenna. "Do you want some ice or something to drink or—"

Jenna forced a laugh. "Laurel, it's okay. Don't worry about it."

"I just feel so, so bad," Laurel continued. Her hands fluttered nervously in the air. "I'm so bad at sports, I don't know what I was *thinking*—"

"Chill," Brittany ordered as she walked back into the rec room. "It's not Jenna's job to make you feel better right now."

Jenna flashed Laurel an extra smile. Brittany could always be counted on to tell it like it was, but sometimes, Jenna secretly thought, Brittany could *try* to be a little nicer. It wouldn't kill her—especially since they'd known Laurel for only a few months. She had moved to Lewisville in the middle of the school year, and even though she'd made friends pretty quickly, Jenna secretly suspected that Laurel still felt like the new kid. That would be one explanation for why she was always scurrying around, so quick to say "Yes!" or "Sorry!" like she thought she was about to lose all her friends.

"Here, Jenna," Maggie said, holding out a T-shirt.

"Thanks," Jenna said. She turned to face the wall as

she pulled off her pajama top and changed into Maggie's T-shirt, careful not to get any blood on the sleeve. Jenna had barely gotten a look at the injury before Brittany slapped a piece of gauze over it.

"I'm applying pressure," Brittany said importantly. "To stop the blood."

"Yes. Thank you," Jenna said, hiding a smile as she took the gauze from Brittany.

"Does it hurt really bad?" Laurel asked anxiously. "I'm so sorry."

"It's okay," Jenna replied. She lifted up a corner of the gauze to peek at the cut. It was bleeding less already. In fact, Jenna thought it didn't look that much worse than a cat scratch. "See? Almost all better. No big deal."

She didn't mention that it still hurt and that the pain was radiating deep into her muscle.

"Oh. That really isn't a big deal," Brittany said. She sounded a little disappointed. "I don't even think you need a Band-Aid."

"Yep. It looks like I'm gonna live," Jenna joked, and all the girls laughed. "Let's go get some—"

There was a sudden silence.

"Um, what?" asked Maggie. "Let's get some what?"

"Shhhhh," Jenna whispered as her face went pale. "Did you guys hear that?"

"Hear what?" asked Laurel, taking a step closer to the other girls.

"I swear I just heard, like, a growling sound or something," Jenna replied softly, holding up her hand. "Just—listen—"

All the girls were quiet, their heads tilted toward the window. And then it came again, a soft *rrrrrrrrrRRRRRRRRRRRRR* that grew to a crescendo and made the hair on the back of Jenna's neck stand up. She looked quickly at her friends and could tell right away, from the scared expression in their eyes, that they had heard it too.

rrrrrrrrrrrrrrrrRRRRRRRRRRRRRRRRRRRRRRRRRR.

Suddenly a shadow darted across the closed curtains. With a sinking feeling in the pit of her stomach, Jenna realized: *There was something outside the window.*

"Did you see that?" she asked hoarsely. She pointed at the window.

"What?" Laurel asked.

But Maggie caught Jenna's eye and nodded.

So she'd seen it too.

13

Jenna crept closer to the window. She pressed herself flat against the wall and waited for something—for the growl to come again, for the shadow to pass by the window once more.

Then she snuck a glance at her friends, all huddled together in the middle of the room.

"I'm going to open the curtains," Jenna whispered.

"No! Don't!" Laurel begged.

"I have to," Jenna replied. "We need to know what's out there." She glanced at Maggie and Brittany, but neither one met her gaze. That's when Jenna knew that she was on her own.

She took a deep breath, mentally counted to three—*one, two, three*—and yanked open the curtains to see what was roaming around out there in the middle of the night.

She came face-to-face with a dark, hulking form on the other side of the window. Nothing but a thin pane of glass separated them.

CHAPTER 3

As the creature slammed against the window, everyone screamed so loudly that Jenna couldn't even hear her own voice in all the commotion. She raced back to the middle of the room, where her friends were frozen in fear.

Then the door banged open, and the room was flooded with light.

"Girls! Girls! What on earth is going on?" Maggie's mom, Mrs. Marcuzzi, cried.

"There's a monster out there!" Maggie shrieked, pointing at the window.

Mrs. Marcuzzi sighed heavily as she strode across the room.

"No, Mom, don't—" Maggie begged.

But Mrs. Marcuzzi was already at the window. "It's

Rocko!" she exclaimed, and started to laugh. "Lou?" she called to Maggie's dad. "The Jacobsons' dog got out again."

"Oh, for Pete's sake." Mr. Marcuzzi's voice came from the hallway. "I'll take him home."

"Here, Dad," Maggie spoke up. "You want my flashlight?"

"Rocko's a big dog, but he's nothing to be afraid of," Mrs. Marcuzzi said to the girls. "You know that, Maggie."

"Mom, have you *seen* Rocko's teeth?" Maggie argued. "They're huge. And he's all slobbery. Besides, we didn't *know* it was only Rocko."

"Yeah," added Laurel. "What if it was the—the Marked Monster?"

As Mrs. Marcuzzi laughed again, Brittany shot Laurel a dirty look. This time, Jenna was with Brittany. Laurel should've known better than to say that. Now Mrs. Marcuzzi was going to go all *Mom* on them.

"The Marked Monster! Are those stories still going around?" Mrs. Marcuzzi said, shaking her head. "I haven't thought about the Marked Monster in ages."

"It's just a stupid story Jenna told," Brittany said.

"What do you know about the Marked Monster, Mrs. M.?" Jenna asked.

"Maybe I'll tell you girls over breakfast," Mrs. Marcuzzi replied. "But I don't see any reason to scare you more than you already are."

Suddenly everyone heard a loud *thud* from outside, and the sound of Mr. Marcuzzi shouting. With a look of alarm, Mrs. Marcuzzi ran over to the window, with the girls following right behind her.

Mr. Marcuzzi had fallen backward in the mud, and Rocko had jumped up on him and was covering his face with slobbery dog kisses!

"Oh no. This is not good," Mrs. Marcuzzi said, but even she had to laugh. Maggie and her mom had the same loud, infectious laugh—just like they had the same dark, curly hair—and the sound always made Jenna laugh even harder. "Maggie, I'm going to go outside and help your dad. I think this calls for some hot chocolate— what do you think, girls? Sound good?"

"I'm on it," Maggie said through her giggles. "Come on—we have marshmallows *and* whipped cream!"

"What's going on?" Maggie's little sister, Sarah, asked from the hallway as she rubbed her eyes sleepily.

"Nothing. Go back to bed," Maggie said rudely as she walked right past Sarah.

"Rocko got out and scared your sister and her friends," Mrs. Marcuzzi explained, "so Daddy's trying to put him on a leash and take him home. But Maggie is right. You need to go back to bed, sweetie."

"Well, I *was* in bed, but they woke me up," Sarah complained. "Now I can't sleep."

Mrs. Marcuzzi sighed. "Go to the kitchen," she said. "The girls are going to make some hot chocolate. A cup of warm milk will help you get back to sleep."

Sarah flashed Maggie a smug grin as she joined the rest of the girls in the hallway.

"Mom. No," Maggie said firmly. "You *promised*. This is *my* sleepover. Sarah is *not* allowed to crash it!"

"It's just five minutes," Mrs. Marcuzzi said. "I've got to go out to help your father with that dog. Go. And don't fight."

Maggie sighed heavily as she stormed off to the kitchen. Jenna followed behind her, smiling a little at Sarah as she passed her. As usual, Jenna felt torn when Maggie and Sarah started fighting. On the one hand, Maggie was Jenna's best friend, so of course she was always going to take her side—no matter what.

But on the other hand, Jenna was a little sister

too—so she knew where Sarah was coming from. Jenna's big brother, Jason, was always ordering Jenna to go to her room or stop bugging him, even if she was minding her own business, like reading a magazine in the living room while he played video games with his friends. It was totally unfair, but at this point, Jenna was used to it.

Besides, it wasn't like she had some burning desire to play Alien Robot Kung Fu Attackers with Jason and the guys. Jenna imagined it had to be even worse for Sarah, who would obviously *love* to get her nails painted and hang out with the older girls at the sleepover.

But if Maggie didn't want Sarah around, Jenna wasn't going to argue with her about it. That wouldn't stop Jenna from giving Sarah some marshmallows from her hot chocolate, though. She could do that much, at least.

In the kitchen, Maggie got out a large glass pitcher and filled it with milk. Then she started heating it in the microwave while she searched for the hot chocolate mix in the pantry. "Got it!" she finally announced. "Jenna? Can you get the whipped cream out of the fridge?"

"Sure thing," Jenna replied.

Sarah perched on one of the tall stools at the island in the middle of the kitchen. "I want marshmallows and whipped cream on my hot chocolate!" she announced.

"Well, you're not getting them," Maggie said as the microwave beeped. She pulled the pitcher of hot milk out and poured some into a mug. "I believe Mom said that some 'warm milk'—*not* hot chocolate with whipped cream and marshmallows—would help you get back to sleep."

As Brittany started to giggle, a look of outrage crossed Sarah's face.

"Oh, who cares, Maggie?" Jenna asked quickly as she dumped a spoonful of chocolate powder into Sarah's mug. Then she leaned over and whispered into Maggie's ear, "Don't give her a reason to make a scene and get your mom all mad at us." Maggie just nodded, but Jenna could tell that she saw her point.

The rest of the girls loaded up their hot chocolate with marshmallows and whipped cream, just as Mr. and Mrs. Marcuzzi walked back in the front door.

"I swear, if they don't fix their fence soon—" Mr. Marcuzzi was saying.

"Well, it was the right thing to do, bringing Rocko back," interrupted Mrs. Marcuzzi. "It's not safe for a dog to wander around in the middle of the night like that. What if he got hit by a car?"

"Maybe they could fix their fence already," Mr. Marcuzzi said, walking into the kitchen with Mrs. Marcuzzi. Jenna tried not to smile at the mud that was splattered all over his clothes. "Then Rocko wouldn't get out at all."

"Hey, Dad," Maggie called out. "You want some hot chocolate?"

"Uh, no thanks, kiddo," Mr. Marcuzzi replied. "Shouldn't you girls be getting back to bed?"

"Yeah, we will," Maggie replied. "We just wanted to make sure you got Rocko home and everything."

"And didn't get caught by the Marked Monster!" cracked Brittany.

"The Marked Monster?" asked Sarah, perking up. "What's that?"

"It's *nothing*," Mrs. Marcuzzi, giving the older girls a look that told them to keep quiet. "Sarah. Back to bed. Now."

"But I—"

"*Now.*"

Still grumbling, Sarah slid off the stool and trudged back to her room. When Mrs. Marcuzzi's voice sounded like that, *nobody* argued with her.

"The rest of you, try to keep it down, okay?" Mrs. Marcuzzi asked with a smile. "You don't have to go to sleep, but you can't keep everyone else up."

"Yes, Mrs. Marcuzzi," Maggie's friends replied in unison.

"Let's go up to my room," Maggie said. "We can finish our hot chocolate there." The other girls followed Maggie up the stairs and through the hall to her bedroom.

"So what do you want to do now?" Laurel asked. "More scary stories?"

"No, I'm sick of scary stories," Brittany said. "How about we—"

"Jenna! Your arm!" Maggie suddenly exclaimed.

Everyone turned to stare at Jenna's arm. Bright red blood was soaking through the sleeve of Maggie's T-shirt.

"Oh no! I'm sorry, Maggie!" Jenna exclaimed. "I didn't realize it had started bleeding again. Ugh, look at all this blood on your shirt!"

"Don't worry about it," Maggie said. "Brit, where's the first-aid kit?"

"I left it downstairs," Brittany replied. "I guess you needed that Band-Aid after all, Jenna. I'll go grab some."

"Yeah," Jenna replied. "I guess so." She twisted her neck to get a better look at the cut. It had started throbbing again as blood oozed down her arm, and the smell of the blood—thick, with a metallic tang—filled Jenna's nose.

She wasn't usually the type to get grossed out by the sight of blood. But this cut wasn't usual, either. It was almost like it could stop—and start—bleeding at will. Jenna's blood started to clot; she could see it in glob form, thick and gelatinous. It would quiver if she touched it.

She closed her eyes.

"Jenna?" Laurel's voice sounded very far away.

"Jenna! You should sit!" Maggie said urgently, pushing Jenna down onto the bed. "Are you okay?"

Jenna shook her head, as if to clear it. "Sorry. I just got kind of light-headed there for a second."

When Brittany returned, she didn't say anything as she carefully placed a square of sterile gauze over the cut and wrapped it with medical tape. "There," she said, examining her work. "That should help."

"Thanks," Jenna replied, grateful for Brittany's take-charge attitude.

"You should take it easy," Brittany said seriously. "Just rest and relax so that your cut will stop bleeding."

"Weird cut, huh?" Jenna said, looking at the bandage. "It didn't *seem* like a big deal."

"Yeah," Brittany agreed. "It must be deeper than it looks. Or maybe that's just what happens when you get *marked by the Marked Monster!*"

Brittany said that last part in such a funny, spooky-sounding voice that everyone started to laugh.

"Oh, because of the claw, you mean?" Jenna asked, suddenly feeling anxious, but forcing herself to laugh too. "Yeah, I guess you're right. I guess I did get marked by the Marked Monster!"

Brittany turned back to the other girls. "We should watch another movie now," she announced. "So that Jenna can chill and hopefully this cut can stop bleeding already. We wouldn't want the Marked Monster lured here by the smell of blood!"

"Gross," Maggie said, wrinkling up her nose. "No offense, Jenna. You know I love you, even when your arm starts bleeding all over my shirt."

"I'm really sorry about that," Jenna said again.

"Jenna! Forget it. I'm just messing with you," replied Maggie.

"I'm ready for a movie," Laurel spoke up.

"Don't think that watching a movie now will get you out of Truth or Dare later," Brittany said, waggling her finger in Laurel's direction. Everyone laughed again; it was no secret that shy Laurel *hated* Truth or Dare. She could never decide between picking a dare or promising to tell the truth—probably because she knew that Brittany saved the worst dares and questions just for her.

"I'm ready for a movie too," Jenna spoke up, grinning at her friends. She knew the goofy comedy Maggie had rented would be just the thing to take her mind off that stupid cut.

And the creepy feeling she got whenever she thought about the way that huge, growling dog had shown up right after she got it.

And the way she'd felt a cold wave of fear when Brittany said that she had been marked . . . marked by the Marked Monster.

A few hours later, everyone else was asleep.

Everyone except Jenna.

She lay on the floor, in her aqua sleeping bag, with her favorite pillow scrunched under her head, and listened to the stillness of the house. It was always so strange, the sounds an unfamiliar house made in the middle of the night—soft clicks and sighs, the rattle of the radiators as hot water gurgled through them, the humming of the fridge as it kicked into a cold-air cycle. Quiet sounds that Jenna never noticed during the day, or at her own house.

But now, in the middle of the night, with everyone else fast asleep, those noises seemed louder than ever.

Jenna sighed quietly and tried to roll onto her left side—but a burning pain in her arm immediately reminded her why that wasn't an option. For her entire life she'd been sleeping on her left side. And now she couldn't, all thanks to that stupid scratch from that stupid claw. Jenna was starting to wish she'd never found the stupid thing.

It was official: She couldn't sleep. Jenna decided to close her eyes and count backward from one hundred. It had worked before, when she found herself sleepless in the middle of the night. Maybe it would work tonight.

One hundred, she thought.

Ninety-nine.

Ninety-eight.

Ninety—

No warning for it, but the feeling of falling so fast that screaming wasn't an option, because there was no air left in her lungs—

Wait. Where am I?

It is so dark here.

And so quiet.

Nothing moves, not the grass, not the leaves, not even my—

What was that?

Eyes watching.

Waiting.

Run away.

Run, Jenna, run, run, run!

But she was falling again, falling down and—and—

It was a mouth, a wide-open mouth, waiting to catch her, with fangs that would pierce and teeth that would rip, and oh, it's going to hurt me. Someone help me! Anyone? Anyone?

The sound of her own voice, screaming, shattered the thin veil between dream and reality, so that Jenna, in her terror, could no longer tell which was which. The only thing she knew was that the danger was pressing down on her, and that she could not escape.

It had marked her as its very own.

CHAPTER 4

Strong hands grabbed Jenna's shoulders and shook her; shook her hard. She could hear voices, calling her name—distantly, at first; and then closer—right in her ears—

"Jenna! Jenna, wake up!"

Jenna opened her eyes and immediately closed them again. The overhead light was on, and it seemed . . . unnaturally bright. Blinding, even.

"Jenna!" Maggie said in an urgent whisper. "Wake up!"

Again, the hands shaking her shoulders, ripping her out of the dream and bringing her back to a familiar place. A safe place.

Jenna took a deep breath and opened her eyes.

Three pairs of eyes stared back at her, all filled with concern. And . . . fear?

As she exhaled, Jenna pushed herself up on shaky arms. "I'm sorry," she said with a waver in her voice. "What happened? I had some kind of . . . nightmare, I think. . . ."

"Yeah, you just started screaming, and it was really freaky," Maggie said in a rush. "You know how deeply you sleep—"

Jenna nodded. It was an old joke that she could sleep through just about anything—thunderstorms, fireworks, even an earthquake when her family went to California for a vacation one summer.

"Well, it was really hard to wake you up," Maggie finished. She glanced over her shoulder at the door. "I'm kind of expecting my mom to charge in here any second now."

"That bad?" Jenna asked, grimacing.

No one said anything, but from the looks on their faces, Jenna could figure out the answer to her question.

"Jenna?" Laurel asked. "Do you . . . remember? What you were dreaming about?"

A frown flickered across Jenna's face. "Oh. It was so stupid," she began, taking another deep breath in hopes of quieting her pounding heart. She forced herself to laugh. "Guys, I had a dream about . . . the Marked Monster!"

She laughed again, but no one else did.

"It's kind of funny, actually," she pressed on. "I don't remember all of it, but I think I was back in the clearing in the woods—well, no, actually, I was falling, but at some point I was in the clearing, and then when I was falling again, it was like the Marked Monster was going to, I don't know, *catch* me in its mouth or something. What's up with that, right? Totally bizarre!"

Suddenly Brittany joined in Jenna's laughter. "Jenna! You freaked yourself out with your own story!"

"No!" Jenna said. "I'm not freaked out. It was just a stupid dream."

"I don't know, Jenna," Brittany teased, her blue-gray eyes twinkling with mischief. "You sound pretty scared to me."

"Whatever. It was a scary nightmare, but I'm not scared now."

"If you say so," Brittany said in that same singsong voice she used whenever she teased people. It drove Jenna crazy—just as it had all the years she'd known Brittany. And in a sudden flash, Jenna was willing to do just about anything to make Brittany shut up.

"Well, if I was scared, would I suggest we camp out

in the clearing next weekend?" Jenna said loudly.

"Shhh!" Maggie whispered, glancing at the door again.

Jenna lowered her voice as she continued. "Seriously, guys, let's do it! Let's camp out in the clearing behind my house. We can solve the mystery of the Marked Monster once and for all!"

"What mystery?" Laurel asked.

"You know, if it exists or not," Jenna said, and the more she spoke, the more excited she started to feel. "You heard Mrs. Marcuzzi. This story's been around forever. We can camp out in the *exact spot* where I found the claw, and we'll stay up all night and see if we can find the Marked Monster. Maybe Jason will let me borrow his camera!"

"Keep dreaming," Maggie said with a laugh. Jenna rolled her eyes, even though Maggie was probably right. Jason *never* let her borrow his stuff—especially not the fancy video camera he'd gotten for his birthday.

"Forget Jason, we can just take a video with my cell phone if the Marked Monster shows up," Brittany said, holding up her shiny pink phone.

Maggie and Jenna exchanged a smile as Maggie subtly flashed four fingers at Jenna. Brittany was the first one of their friends to get a cell phone; she mentioned her cell so often that Jenna and Maggie had started keeping track. This was the fourth time tonight.

"I'm in," Maggie said.

"Really?" Laurel asked. "I don't know about camping out, guys. Why don't we just, like, sleep over at Jenna's house?"

"Oh, Laurel, you'll love it!" Jenna exclaimed. "We camp out every summer in this clearing behind my house that's surrounded by these *enormous* pine trees. You, like, can't even see civilization when you're there. It's *awesome*."

"Yeah!" Maggie chimed in. "We roast marshmallows, and Jenna's mom grills up the best hot dogs, and then we stay up really, really late and watch for shooting stars."

"That does sound cool," Laurel replied slowly. "It's just . . . I've never been camping before. I don't have any camping stuff."

"Don't worry about it," Brittany announced. "You can borrow anything you need from me."

"You really don't need anything besides your sleeping bag," Jenna added. "And maybe a flashlight. I have a tent and a tarp and everything already."

Laurel smiled. "Okay," she gave in. "I'll be there."

"Excellent," Jenna said. "Next Friday night. Best-case scenario? We find proof that the Marked Monster really exists. Worst-case scenario? We have an awesome campout."

"Uh, Jenna," Laurel said, "I think you might have those reversed."

Everyone laughed, until Maggie's laugh turned into a yawn so big that her jaw cracked. "Let's go back to sleep," she said. "I'm so tired I can't even think anymore."

No one argued as Maggie turned off the light, and soon the room was dark and quiet as one by one, the girls drifted off to sleep.

Jenna listened to the calm, even breathing of her friends as she made a mental list of everything she had to do before the campout. *I'll ask Mom and Dad's permission when I get home tomorrow,* she thought drowsily. *And get the tent out of the basement to air it out. And make a list of snack stuff to buy. And . . .*

Before she could finish her thought, Jenna drifted off to sleep. But even as she slept, the nighttime noises wove themselves into her dreams. From the creaking of tree limbs blown by the wind to the thin screech of branches scraping across the windows. There was something troubling the deepest parts of Jenna's mind, something that was trying to warn her.

If only there was a way for Jenna to understand.

In the morning, everything seemed normal—from the sun streaming through the window to the sleepy yawns from girls who had gotten only a few hours of sleep the night before. It was easy, in that bright morning sunshine, for Jenna to think only about the fun parts of camping . . . and not the creature that had left its claw in the clearing. She stood in front of the mirror above Maggie's dresser as she pulled her short blond hair into a low ponytail. Jenna had cut her hair over winter break, and it still hadn't grown back to a length where it could comfortably fit into a ponytail, but every day she tried. And every day she wound up with a tiny little ponytail gathered at the top of her neck.

"Hey, Maggie, I'm gonna take your shirt home to wash it and get that blood stain out," Jenna called across the room, where her friend was already peeling the polish off her fingernails. It was one of her weirdest quirks—a fresh manicure lasted only a few hours before Maggie started attacking it.

"Don't be ridiculous. Just throw it in the hamper," Maggie replied, not looking up. "My mom can do it."

"Jenna, don't forget your claw!" Brittany said loudly, pointing across the room.

"Yeah, seriously don't forget that," Maggie added, laughing.

"Oh, I would never," Jenna said. "Because after we prove that the Marked Monster is really out there, I'm going to sell it online for big money."

"You wish!" Brittany cracked.

"Hey, what time does the library open today?" Laurel asked.

"Noon," Maggie replied. "Are you working on your history project?"

Laurel nodded. "My research is almost done, but I haven't even *started* the poster yet! I have to find all those visual-aid things. And write captions. And—"

"Stop, stop, stop," Jenna interrupted her, clapping her hands over her ears. "I don't even have a topic yet!"

"Really?" Laurel asked. "You know it's due in, like, a week, right?"

"I know, I know," Jenna groaned. "I just haven't been able to think of a topic. I wish it could be about anything. 'The history of Lewisville and the surrounding area'—come on, like there could be anything more boring than this town."

"A paragraph on your topic is due on Monday!" Maggie said. "That's the day after *tomorrow*."

"Come on, don't make me feel any more stressed out about it," Jenna said. "I'm going to figure out a topic today, and tomorrow I'm going to write the paragraph. Okay?"

"You want to come to the library with me this afternoon?" Laurel asked her.

"I would," Jenna replied as she glanced out the window. "But I'm just not in mood for doing research today. It's too nice outside to spend the day in the library!"

Maggie laughed. "Jenna, at some point you've gotta get started on your project! Listen, I'm going to the library after school on Monday. Come with me. My mom can drive us home after."

"Thanks," Jenna said. "And if anybody has any ideas for a topic that you're not going to use . . ." She slung her backpack over her right arm—the one without the cut. "Bye, everybody!"

She gave one last wave to her friends, then skipped down the stairs two at a time and let herself out the front door. She and Maggie had been best friends since first grade, and she felt nearly as comfortable in Maggie's house as she did in her own. They lived only half a mile apart, too—and Jenna had walked that route so often that she could do it on autopilot. Which was exactly how she got home, turning corners without really thinking about where she was going. Jenna wanted to forget about what a big fuss her friends had made about the history project, but their words repeated in her mind. *I'll go ahead and get started today,* she promised herself. *Hopefully I can at least think of a topic that won't completely put me to sleep.*

When Jenna got home, the front door was locked, and both her parents' cars were gone. She fished the key out of her pocket and opened the front door. The house was quiet and cool inside.

"Hello?" she called out. "Anybody home?"

Silence.

But that was to be expected. Jenna's mom was a doctor who often worked nights and weekends in the local hospital's emergency room. Every Saturday morning Mr. Walker ran errands—that must be what he was doing now. As for Jason? Well, Jenna didn't know where he was. Ever since he'd started high school last September, Jason seemed to have a lot of secrets.

At least it's quiet around here today, Jenna thought. *Hopefully I can get some work done since Jason's not hogging the computer.*

After she dumped her backpack and sleeping bag in her bedroom, she went back to the den to turn on the computer. While it was warming up, she poured herself a glass of orange juice in the kitchen. Then she noticed the box of cat food on top of the fridge. *I hope Mom remembered to feed the stray cat last night,* she thought. Just in case her mother had forgotten, Jenna decided to put a little extra food outside. She didn't want the poor cat to be hungry.

Across the yard, at the old tree stump, she found a pile of dry food—apparently untouched. She frowned. It wasn't like the cat to miss a meal. "Here, kitty, kitty," she called softly, though she didn't have high hopes of seeing the little cat, who usually appeared around dusk, just as it was starting to get dark.

SLAM!

A sudden crash shattered the stillness around her. Jenna spun around, her heart pounding.

The back door was closed—and she knew she'd left it open.

It was just the wind, she told herself. *Don't freak out.*

But it wasn't a windy day. In fact, the air was still. Unusually still.

Stop it, Jenna thought fiercely. *Stop freaking out over nothing.*

But she couldn't shake the fear that someone—or something—had closed the door. And with her back to the house, someone—or something—could have entered . . . and she would never know.

At least, not until she went back inside.

Jenna bit her lip as she stared at the back door. She wished, for one fast moment, that her mom and dad were home. She wished that right now her dad was about to mow the lawn and her mom was sitting in the chair by the window, reading a magazine.

But wishing wouldn't make it happen. Jenna was home alone, and she had to go back inside the house.

Alone.

At least, she hoped she would be alone.

She mustered all her courage and walked swiftly across the lawn. She hesitated for only a second before she yanked open the door. She stood in the threshold and called out, "Hello?" as loudly as she could.

She was surprised by how normal her voice sounded. You'd never know that she was so scared.

The same silence that had greeted Jenna when she got home hung in the air. After several seconds in the doorway, she charged back into the house, scolding herself for getting all freaked out over nothing.

Her orange juice was still sitting on the counter. Jenna grabbed the glass and carried it over to the computer station in the den. *I'll just check my e-mail for one minute,* she thought. *And then I'll really get to work.*

But right after Jenna entered her password, she heard a sound that made her freeze.

Thunk-scraaaaaaaaaaaaaaaaaaape.

Thunk-scraaaaaaaaaaaaaaaaaaape.

Thunk-scraaaaaaaaaaaaaaaaaaape.

The sound was coming from the hallway.

There was no denying it, Jenna realized, as cold goose bumps covered her entire body. Something was in the house, making some mysterious, horrifying noise, unlike anything she had ever heard before.

And it was coming closer!

CHAPTER 5

Can I get to the door? Jenna wondered wildly. *The front door, the back door, a window—can I get out of here?*

She didn't know what to do.

Thunk-scraaaaaaaaaaaaaaaaaape.

If only she could figure out *where*, exactly, it was coming from—the front of the hall or the back of the hall—maybe, Jenna thought, she had a chance to get out. A chance to escape. All she had to do was pick the right door.

But there was no more time to think. She had to make a decision. She had to move, *fast*—

Before it was too late.

Without making a noise, Jenna crept through the den, hugging the wall as if she could make herself invisible. All too soon she found herself at the entrance to the den. She had to decide—front door or back—and pray that she didn't make the wrong choice.

Taking a deep breath, she dashed into the hall.

A scream stopped her in her tracks.

"*Jason?*" she exclaimed.

"Jenna! What—what—" her brother sputtered.

Jenna started to laugh. "Did I scare you?"

"No!"

"Because you seem kind of, you know, *scared*," Jenna teased him. "Or at least *startled*."

"I didn't know you were home, okay?" Jason answered. "All of a sudden you came sprinting out of the den like some—"

"Sorry I *scared* you," Jenna replied, smirking. It wasn't often that she had the chance to tease Jason as mercilessly as he usually teased her.

Then she took a closer look at her brother, and her eyes grew wide. "Jason? *What* are you doing?"

"Nothing," he said shortly. But the red blush creeping up his neck gave him away.

Jenna's eyes flitted over the stretchy elastic sweatband pulled across Jason's forehead, and the four heavy cement blocks he was dragging down the hallway.

"Let me guess," she said as she started to giggle. "You're going to build some kind of wood-and-cement thing that you will try to smash with your bare hands. Are you playing *Karate Kid* or something?"

"Why don't you mind your own business?" Jason snapped as he yanked the sweatband off his head.

"No, no, Jason, it's cool," Jenna said, laughing. "If you want to work on your martial arts, don't let me stand in your way. But you might want to find something instead of those cement blocks. Dad's going to use them to build a barbecue pit out back."

"Yeah, he's been saying that for, what, three years now?" Jason asked.

Jenna and Jason grinned at each other for a moment.

"When did you get home, anyway?" he asked her.

Jenna shrugged. "A little while ago," she replied. "I went outside to feed the cat and—hey, was that you who closed the door on me?"

"Sorry. I didn't see you," said Jason.

"How could you?" Jenna said. "Not with that sweatband covering your eyes!"

This time Jason ignored Jenna's teasing. He pushed past her and went into the den, where he plunked himself down at the computer and started swigging her juice.

"Is this your e-mail?" he asked as a wicked smile crossed his face. "I wonder what MagPie13 has to say?"

"Jason! No!" Jenna shrieked as she ran over to the computer. "Mind your own business!"

"'Hey, Jenna,'" he read. "'You left your claw here. I'm gonna drop it off on the way to the mall because I don't want the Marked Monster coming here to look for you!'"

"Quit it, loser!" Jenna yelled as she elbowed Jason's hand off the mouse. Instantly she closed her e-mail.

But it was too late.

"Whoa, whoa, whoa," Jason said. "What is old MagPie talking about? What is this *claw*?"

"It's nothing—just this thing I found in the woods," Jenna said with a shrug. "I told a scary story last night about the Marked Monster, and I used the claw as a prop. No big deal."

"Ooh, the Marked Monster!" he sang out. "Spooooky!"

"What do you know about it?" Jenna asked, curious in spite of herself.

"What, that it's a stupid legend somebody thought up to scare babies like you?" Jason teased. "What else is there to know?"

"Yeah, exactly," Jenna said. "Move," she ordered him, plunking down on the edge of the computer chair as she tried to push him out of it. "I need the computer."

"Too bad," Jason said, smirking as he clicked an icon for one of his video games. "I was here first."

"You were not!" she cried. "You were in the hall grunting like a pig as you dragged those stupid cement blocks to your room! Come on, Jason. I have homework."

"You have homework? Please." He laughed. "Just wait until you get to high school. *Then* you'll know what it means to have homework."

"Come on," Jenna begged. "Please! I have so much work to do on my history project for Mrs. Ramirez. You know Mom always says that homework comes before video games!"

"Whoa, I remember that project. It was *hard*. What's your topic?"

"I don't have one yet," she admitted. "What was yours?"

"Farming in the 1800s," Jason remembered. "There were a bunch of old diaries in the Lewisville Archives at the library. Man, those people had it rough. They almost ran out of food one year when the crops didn't do well."

"You're still sitting in my chair," Jenna reminded him.

"Here you go, moron," her brother said as he stood up from the computer chair. "Have fun with your research. I just realized I better get those cement blocks out of the hallway before Mom gets home from the hospital."

In the doorway, Jason paused. "Maybe you should do your report on the Marked Monster," he called over his shoulder.

"Thanks. Great idea," Jenna said sarcastically. "Actually, I mean *garbage* idea. I don't want to get an F."

"Whatever. It's part of the town's history," Jason shot back. "Excuse me for giving you an awesome topic that won't bore you to death."

With that, he disappeared into the hall, and once again Jenna heard:

Thunk-scraaaaaaaaaaaaaaaaaape.

Thunk-scraaaaaaaaaaaaaaaaaape.

Thunk-scraaaaaaaaaaaaaaaaaape.

She scrambled out of her chair and ran to the hallway. "Jas?"

When he looked up from the cement blocks, Jenna could see little beads of sweat dotting his red face. "What?" he asked.

"You really think the Marked Monster would be a good topic for my project?"

"I don't know. Yeah," he said. "Haven't the legends about the Marked Monster been passed down for, like, two hundred years or something?"

"That long?"

"Something like that. And I remember reading in one of the diaries that the town council passed a law that nobody could build or plant crops in the Sacred Square."

"The *what*?" Jenna said, raising her eyebrows.

"I don't remember exactly, but there was a place in the town called the Sacred Square, and this new settler wanted to build a cabin on it, and everybody got all upset and called an emergency meeting about it," Jason said, wrinkling his forehead as he tried to remember. "And it was because of an old superstition about the Marked Monster. Some Native American deal with the creature or something."

"Wow. That sounds really cool," Jenna said thoughtfully.

"I'm waiting."

"Waiting for what?"

"An apology," Jason replied smugly. "Weren't you just

making fun of my project idea for you?"

"Yes. Yes, I was," Jenna said. "I'm sorry, Karate Kid. You were right and I was wrong."

"Shut up."

"Sorry, Sensei. I apologize, Master. Please, Sensei, accept my most humble apologies."

"Shut up, moron."

"Yes, Sensei. I'll shut up now, Sensei."

Jason slammed the door on his way into his bedroom, which made Jenna laugh even harder. She sat down at the computer and typed "Marked Monster in Lewisville" into a search engine. It took half a second for a dozen links to flash onto the screen. Jenna's curiosity about the Marked Monster grew with every link she clicked on. *This is going to be an amazing topic,* she thought—even though she hated to admit that her brother had been right. *I want to know* everything *about the Marked Monster!*

As she sat there, learning more from each link, Jenna had no idea how much she would regret it.

At dinner that night, Jenna's dad had one question for her: "How is that history project coming?"

"Great, actually!" Jenna replied with a big grin. She'd spent the entire afternoon glued to the computer, scribbling down all kinds of notes for the report she had to write. She definitely had enough background information to write the summary paragraph that was due on Monday. "I finally have an awesome topic, and it's really interesting. Is it okay if I go to the library with Maggie after school on Monday? Her mom can drive us home."

Jenna's parents beamed at her. "Of course it is, sweetie!" her mom said. "Tell me all about your topic!"

Jason cleared his throat loudly, but Jenna chose to ignore him. "It's about the history of the legend of the Marked Monster," she replied. "And how it affected our town and the early settlers and stuff."

"Hang on a minute," Mr. Walker spoke up. "You can't write up a spooky story and call it a history project."

"No, I'm going to focus on the historical parts," Jenna said quickly. "I mean, I'm going to do a lot more research at the library, but I already learned that there was a section of town where nobody was allowed to live because of the Marked Monster. So this legend actually affected how the town was formed."

"Oh, okay," her dad said, looking relieved. "That's

fascinating, Jenna. I think your teacher will really like that approach."

"A-*hem!*" Jason cleared his throat again, louder.

"You're not getting sick, are you?" Dr. Walker asked him.

"No," Jason grumbled. "But just so you know, I gave Jenna the idea for her project."

"Thank you, Jason," Dr. Walker said, smiling at him. "It makes me so happy when you two get along and help each other out."

Across the table, Jenna glared at her brother. It was *so* like him to insist on getting credit for every little thing! And just when her mom and dad were acting like they were proud of her, instead of disappointed that she'd brought home yet another B-minus.

"Actually, I started researching the Marked Monster last week," Jenna said, which was true. Her parents didn't need to know it was in preparation for her sleepover story. "Before Jason said anything about it."

"Well, let me know if you need any help with your project, honey," Dr. Walker said. "I can pick up some supplies for your poster on the way home from the hospital tomorrow, if you want."

"Thanks, Mom," Jenna replied. "That would be great. Oh, before I forget—is it okay if I have a campout on Friday night? With Maggie and Brittany and Laurel?"

"I don't see why not," Dr. Walker replied. "Keep an eye on the weather, though—just in case we get a late cold spell."

"Thank you!" Jenna exclaimed. Then she paused, straining her ears to hear something outside, a scraping noise so faint that she couldn't be sure she'd heard it at all. "Do you hear that?"

"What?" asked Dr. Walker.

"It sounds like a . . . like a scratching sound?" Jenna said with a slight frown. "Coming from outside?"

Her parents shook their heads. "It's probably that stray cat," Mr. Walker said. "The one you've been feeding."

"I don't think so," Jenna said as she walked over to the window. "It never comes up to the house. I wish it would. I'd love to have a cat!"

She peered out the window, but it was so dark she couldn't see anything. She turned back to her family. "So what's for dessert?"

"I bought a pie at the supermarket this morning," Mr. Walker said.

"Pie again?" Jason complained. "Why don't you ever get cake?"

"We *always* have cake," argued Jenna.

"And that's why I bought a pie today," Mr. Walker said. "Would you please serve dessert, Jenna? Jason, you can clear the table tonight."

In the kitchen, Jenna set out four dessert plates and took the pie out of the box. "Cherry!" she exclaimed. "Thanks, Dad!"

"Hey, I remembered your favorite kind of pie!"

"Do we have ice cream?" she called out to the dining room.

"Hey, I remembered what you like to put on top of your favorite kind of pie!" Mr. Walker joked.

Jenna did a fist pump as she opened the freezer. But even though she searched through every shelf, she couldn't find the carton of ice cream anywhere.

"Looking for something?" Jason asked with a sly grin as he set a stack of dirty dishes in the sink.

"Yeah, Dad says he bought ice cream, but I can't find it."

"Oh. That's my bad," Jason said, still grinning. "But it was a delicious afternoon snack."

"You ate the *whole thing*?" Jenna asked.

"I was really hungry," he replied with a shrug. "It was so good—cold and creamy and sweet. French vanilla, *mmmm*."

"I hate you so much."

"Likewise."

As he passed her, Jason reached out and lightly flicked Jenna on the arm. A searing pain shot through her arm, all the way to her wrist. She gasped and grabbed her arm. The knife she'd been holding to cut the pie clattered to the floor. "Mom!" she yelled.

"What's going on in there?" Dr. Walker called.

"Nothing," Jason said quickly—too quickly. He leaned over to Jenna and hissed, "Don't be such a baby. I barely touched you."

Jenna opened her mouth to retort, but stopped short. She knew that Jason was telling the truth.

So why did it hurt so much?

Suddenly she remembered—the cut she had received the night before. It hadn't done much healing, apparently.

Just then Dr. Walker appeared in the kitchen. "Well? What's going on?"

"Jason ate all the ice cream," Jenna said.

Dr. Walker sighed. "Jason, was that really necessary?"

"It's got lots of calcium," he pointed out.

"So does yogurt! Honestly, you're old enough to know better than to eat an entire carton of ice cream."

"Sorry, Mom."

"And also he flicked me," Jenna said. She couldn't help herself. "Right in my arm."

"Unacceptable, Jason," Dr. Walker said. "I think you can miss your karate lesson on Monday."

"Mom! No! Come on, I have a match next Saturday! I *have* to be at the lesson or Sensei will be so mad!"

Dr. Walker shook her head. "Maybe you can use the time to try to understand why you're still picking on your little sister."

"Thanks, Jenna," he snapped. "Thanks a lot."

"You're welcome," she said sweetly as she took a big bite out of her slice of pie. Jason hardly ever got busted for being so mean to her, so Jenna was going to enjoy it while she could.

CHAPTER 6

After school on Monday, Jenna and Maggie walked to the public library. It was already filling up with students from the high school and the middle school, all working furiously on the big projects that were due before school let out for the summer. The girls went straight to the very back, where the Lewisville Archives were located. After Jenna pulled open the heavy oak door, Maggie flipped on the lights.

Walking into the archives was like stepping through a time machine. Oil paintings of the town's founder and mayors glared from the walls; in the oldest portraits, the men wore powdered white wigs and formal, old-fashioned suits. Tattered maps and stained surveyor's charts that chronicled the town's growth had been framed and mounted on the walls in places of honor. There were bookcases throughout the room, each one crammed with old, leather-bound volumes filled with yellowed pages. One bookcase contained the minutes from every town council meeting since 1812.

The room was steeped in history. Jenna could feel it all around her; she could even smell it in the stuffy, dusty air.

"I'd kill for a computer in here," she whispered to Maggie, not even realizing that she'd dropped her voice to a hush. "This is going to be impossible. How am I going to find *anything* about the Marked Monster? Like I really want to sift through all this stuff! There must be, like, a thousand books in here!"

"And who knows if anybody even wrote anything down about the Marked Monster in the town records?" Maggie pointed out. "What if Jason was just messing with you?"

Jenna paused. She hadn't thought of that.

"It would be so like him!" She groaned as a sudden wave of panic washed over her. "And now it's Monday and I already handed in my paragraph on this topic. How would I ever think of another topic and find enough info to get the project done now?"

Maggie made a sympathetic face. "No, I'm probably wrong. Not even Jason is that evil," she said. "Besides, didn't you say he was bragging to your parents about coming up with the idea?"

"Yeah," Jenna said slowly.

"Well, he wouldn't do that if the whole point was to set you up. I mean, that would make your mom crazy mad, right?"

"*Crazy* mad," Jenna repeated. She was starting to feel a little better. Even Jason was aware of how much her parents were pushing her to do well in school. They would completely freak out if she did poorly on her project because Jason had played a mean prank on her.

But she still faced an enormous stack of books—and no quick way to find the info she needed. "I guess I'd better get to it," she said, sighing, as she pulled a book with a cranberry-colored cover off the shelf. She blew a thick cloud of dust off it. "'Town Records, 1844 to 1845.' Please wake me up if I start snoring."

"Sorry, Jenna, you're on your own," Maggie said with a laugh. "I have to go photocopy a picture of Manfred Lewis for my poster."

"What, you couldn't print that off the Internet?" Jenna asked. "I'm sure the town website has a picture of the founder of Lewisville."

"I could've," Maggie said, smiling slyly. "But then I wouldn't have had a chance to come to the library and use the computer here. And, you know, chat with anybody who's online."

Jenna started laughing. Mrs. Marcuzzi was insanely strict about the Internet. Whenever Maggie was online, Mrs. Marcuzzi always hovered right behind her. Maggie could hardly e-mail or chat with anybody without her mom reading every word.

"Well, if nobody's online, you have to come back and help me," Jenna said. "I don't even know where to begin."

"Sure, sure, I will," Maggie said with a little wave as she drifted out the door. Jenna watched her go and knew that Maggie wasn't going to budge from the library computer until Mrs. Marcuzzi arrived to pick them up in two hours.

Jenna really was on her own.

With a heavy sigh, she sat down at one of the desks. It was made out of shiny dark wood; the top of the desk slanted downward, with a tiny, tarnished keyhole near the edge of the lid. Suddenly filled with curiosity, Jenna tried to open it.

But the desk was locked.

I wonder what's in here, she thought. Why would this desk be locked, in the barely used archives room?

Jenna had almost completely forgotten about her research. All she wanted to do was open that desk and peek inside. Then she remembered the safety pin holding one of her backpack's straps together. *Maybe I can open the lock without the key,* she thought. She'd seen somebody on TV open a lock that way once.

Jenna bit her tongue as she slipped the pin into the keyhole. She jiggled it around, up, down, to the right, to the left. Every few seconds she tried to open the desk, but the lid wouldn't budge.

Five minutes passed like this, and she was just about to give up, when suddenly she heard it.

Click.

The faint sound had come from the lock.

Holding her breath, Jenna tried again to lift the lid.

This time it opened on hinges so creaky the squeak seemed earsplitting—but the lid opened only a couple of inches, not nearly wide enough for her to see if anything was inside. She leaned closer to the desk and tried to peer in it.

"*What* do you think you're doing?"

The voice scared Jenna so much that she jumped up; the lid of the desk banged down, hard, and then she heard a sickening sound—a second thump, as if something inside the desk had come loose, or broken when the lid fell. *Oh my God, did I just break some precious town heirloom or something?* she wondered frantically as she spun around to see an old man glaring at her from the doorway. *I'm going to be in so much trouble!* Jenna tried to hide the safety pin in her hand, but only managed to stab herself in the palm.

"Ow! What—Sorry—I was—"

"Can't you read?" the old man barked. He lifted his cane and banged it on the open door, making Jenna jump again. "Didn't you see the sign? It says 'No Admittance without Permission of the Town Archivist'! That's me. And I don't remember giving you permission to come in here."

"I'm sorry," Jenna said miserably. "I, um, I didn't—"

"Speak up!" the man bellowed. "I can't hear a word you're saying."

This is great, Jenna thought. *Now this old deaf guy is going to yell at me—*

Then she realized something. If he was hard of hearing, maybe he hadn't heard the desk lid fall.

And maybe he hadn't heard whatever had thumped inside it.

"I'm sorry, sir," she said, louder this time. "I, um, I didn't see the sign—"

"You shouldn't be sitting at that desk. And you shouldn't be touching that book without gloves!"

Jenna stood up on shaky legs, blinking quickly so she wouldn't start to cry. She *hated* being yelled at, especially by adults, and *especially* by strangers.

"I honestly didn't see the sign," she repeated. "I was trying to do some research. For this history project—"

The old man sighed. "For Mrs. Ramirez?"

Jenna nodded without saying anything.

"Every year, a parade of middle schoolers traipses through here," he grumbled. "Every year. But you're getting a rather late start, aren't you, young lady?"

She nodded again.

"Well, what's your topic?"

"Um," she replied, starting to blush. "Um. The—the

Marked Monster?" She just *knew* the old man was going to yell at her again—probably for wasting his time.

But she was wrong. To her astonishment, his eyes lit up. "Well!" he exclaimed. "Well! That's a clever choice! Quite the deviation from the standard Blizzard of 1907 that so many students report on, year after year after year. Where would you like to begin?"

"Wait a second," Jenna said. "Do *you* know about the Marked Monster? Like, historical things for my project?"

The man nodded solemnly. "My dear, I know more about the Marked Monster than any person still living."

Something in his voice—Jenna couldn't quite put her finger on it—gave her chills.

"My name is Mr. Carson," he said, tapping his chest. "And you are?"

"Jenna, uh, Jenna Walker."

"Wait there, Jenna," Mr. Carson said. "Don't touch anything. I'll be right back."

Jenna stood awkwardly in the middle of the archives room until the man returned with an enormous portfolio and a pair of soft cotton gloves. "Put these on," he ordered her. "They'll keep the oils and dirt from your hands off the archival materials."

My hands are not *dirty and oily!* Jenna thought—but she put the gloves on without arguing.

"Please, have a seat over here," Mr. Carson continued as he gestured to a long table in the middle of the room. Jenna sat next to him and snuck a peek at him while she pretended to arrange her notebook and note cards on the table. Clouds of white hair puffed up from his head, and this close, it was hard for her not to notice how yellow his teeth were, or the way that the corners of his mouth were crusted over with dried spit.

Then, to her embarrassment, she realized that Mr. Carson was watching her. He'd probably caught her staring. But he said nothing—just nodded his head over to the desk in the corner. The one where Jenna had picked the lock.

"That desk belonged to Manfred Lewis himself, you know."

"Really?" Jenna asked in surprise.

"And the story of the Marked Monster—as it concerns Lewisville—is certainly wrapped up in the story of Manfred Lewis. Of course, what we know of the monster predates Lewis."

"Cool," Jenna said as she started scribbling down every word he said.

"Who can say from where the monster came?" Mr. Carson said, closing his eyes and shaking his head. "Most people these days just dismiss the story of the Marked Monster as a myth—a tale of a bogeyman—that some kid dreamed up years ago and that gets passed down from generation to generation. What they don't know, though, is that the legend of the Marked Monster was around long before this country was even founded. According to the Q'ippicut people, the Marked Monster was a curse, a creature whose very existence was a testament to the power of evil."

Jenna felt cold all over . . . except for her injured arm, which was uncomfortably hot.

"In order to survive, the Q'ippicut forged an uneasy peace with the monster. It wasn't marked back then, you know. They called it *Keuhkkituh*—'Creature of the Black Blood.' You see, the Q'ippicut had been forced to live with—or at least *near*—the creature for centuries. They knew more about its unholy form than anyone. Until a few months ago, you could still see their paintings of it in the caves near Mount Madison if you knew where to look—but then those caves were destroyed."

Jenna nodded, remembering the construction

accident that had caused the caves to collapse. For a while, it had been in the news every day. "What did the cave paintings show?" she asked.

"Diagrams of the monster, mainly," Mr. Carson said. He opened the portfolio and took out a yellowed piece of parchment. On it was a copy of one of the cave drawings. Jenna held her breath as she looked at it; the creature drawn there was so horrible that it defied description. But Mr. Carson tried anyway. "You see what a hybrid it is—a missing link, as it were; part lizard, part bird. And yet the beak is filled with teeth like a mammal, and fangs like a snake. The arms are short compared to the rest of the physique. The wings and tail are also incongruous."

"What about the claws?" Jenna asked. "I don't see the claws."

Mr. Carson looked at her sharply. "How did you know about the claws?"

"I—I don't know. I thought I read that somewhere," she said awkwardly. To be honest, she didn't really know why she thought the creature would have claws. After all, the claw she found in the woods behind her house was nothing. It certainly wasn't one of the Marked Monster's talons. It probably came from a hawk, she had told herself at the time, and it just happened to be the perfect prop for her scary story.

"Yes, the claws are the one area in which this drawing is inaccurate." Mr. Carson sighed. "But—given what happened—I can understand why Lewis left them out."

"Manfred Lewis drew this?" Jenna asked.

"Indeed he did. You see, during the mid-eighteenth century, Lewis enjoyed a classical education at some of Europe's finest institutions. But he longed for adventure and, it must be said, had a rather inflated sense of self. He dreamed of coming to the New World and founding a town. When Lewis identified an uninhabited tract in the central plains region, he set out with a band of extended family and friends. The journey was a perilous one; Lewis's own wife and three youngest children died from fever along the way. But at last the party reached the plains, and Lewis incorporated his very own town— which, of course, he named after himself."

"Lewisville," Jenna said.

Mr. Carson nodded. "The settlers had hardly begun laying the foundations for their homesteads when Chief Onongahkan of the Q'ippicut visited them. Lewis made a grave error in approaching the chief with his weapon raised. But Onongahkan had come in peace. As best he could, the chief tried to warn the settlers. He tried to explain the threat posed by the Keuhkkituh. You see, Lewis had founded the town on the very tract of land the Q'ippicut had dedicated to the Keuhkkituh. The settlers had no way of knowing—or even understanding—the danger they were in."

Here Mr. Carson paused and sighed heavily.

"What happened?" Jenna asked—though part of her didn't want to know.

"Lewis humored the old chief. I suspect that he thought it was all a story to scare away the settlers. But he couldn't have been more wrong . . . and he paid dearly for his mistake. You see, right there in front of everyone, he vowed to protect the town from any 'beasts' that attempted to attack it. It was just weeks later that the stillness of the night was shattered by the Keuhkkituh's cry. And the settlers were still living in tents!

"Lewis set off alone, on foot, armed with a musket. According to his diary, he found the creature in the heart of the forest. As soon as he recovered from his horror at its grotesque appearance, he planned to shoot it in the head. But his musket jammed! He would've been a dead man if the chief had not appeared at that very moment, brandishing a spear and a torch. According to Lewis, Onongahkan heated the spear's blade in the fire of the torch, then struck the Keuhkkituh with what should have been a fatal blow: The chief sliced a four-foot gash through the creature's belly. Black blood poured from its body, and its howls could be heard all the way back at the settlement. Lewis and Onongahkan left it there to die."

"Then what happened?" Jenna asked.

"The next morning the settlers and the members of the Q'ippicut tribe returned to the scene of the attack. The dirt was dark and wet with spilled blood, and vultures perched hungrily in the trees, attracted by the smell, likely. But the creature's body was gone. They searched the woods for five days in hopes of finding it, but it had vanished. There were sightings, from time to time; and all accounts report that a long, puckered wound was now visible on the creature's belly—giving the Keuhkkituh a new name: the Marked Monster."

"So that's why it's called the Marked Monster," Jenna said thoughtfully. "Not because it, like, marks its victims."

Mr. Carson looked uncomfortable. "What I've told you so far is pulled from the historical record," he said slowly. "We have primary documents that chronicle Lewis and Onongahkan's battle with the Keuhkkituh that night—though for the last hundred years, the town record has more or less been scrubbed of this fact by the town council."

"How come?" Jenna asked.

"People can be so shortsighted," Mr. Carson said bitterly. "No one *appreciates* the importance of living in a place steeped in such unique history. Oh no, they're worried that these valuable accounts of our history make a mockery of the town or that the settlers had overdramatized a wolf or other such creature! They'll learn someday. You can ignore the history, but that won't make it disappear. And there are . . . stories . . . about the Marked Monster. Stories that cannot be proven—yet, in their very existence, in their sheer persistence, force us to consider that they may perhaps contain an element of truth."

"What are those stories?" Jenna said, sitting very still.

"Manfred Lewis had a daughter," Mr. Carson said. "Her name was Imogen, and she was fifteen when her father founded Lewisville. Two months after Lewis and Onongahkan attacked the Marked Monster, Imogen went berry picking in the woods. She did not return by nightfall."

"What happened to her?"

There was a pause while Mr. Carson struggled to find the right words. "When her father found her, she was wounded—she had a grave injury to her leg. The flesh had been sliced open nearly to the bone, and Imogen was out of her mind with pain and delirium. Lewis carried her home and began the slow process of nursing her back to health, but Imogen never recovered. Lewis's diary is filled with entries that chronicle not only his anxiety about her health, but the progression of her illness—the wound that would not heal; the way she sat awake all night, wild-eyed with fear, claiming to hear sounds that no one else heard and raving about monsters. In her delirium, Imogen scratched at the walls until her fingers bled."

Jenna's mouth was so dry she had to swallow twice before she could speak. "What—what happened to her?" she asked again.

"One night Lewis was called away to settle a dispute," Mr. Carson said quietly. "When he returned to the cabin that he'd built, the door was hanging from its hinges, and Imogen had vanished. A search party banded together immediately, but Imogen was never found."

"She disappeared?" Jenna asked. "Without a trace?"

Mr. Carson looked uncomfortable. "Well, there was one trace," he replied. "Winter had come to Lewisville, and there were several inches of snow on the ground. The snow in the clearing—the one where Lewis had attacked the Marked Monster—was freshly soaked with blood. A great deal of *red* blood, not the black blood of the Marked Monster. At that time, there was no way for the settlers to know if it was human blood, but if it was, it's safe to assume that, if the blood belonged to Imogen, the young girl had exsanguinated."

"Ex-*what*?"

"Bled to death."

Mr. Carson took one look at Jenna's face and immediately changed his tone. "Now, now, don't be frightened!" he said. "This is just a story. Manfred Lewis wrote *nothing* about it in his diary, except that Imogen disappeared in the night and was not found, despite many searches."

"Then how do you know about it?"

"Rumors. Stories, as I said, passed down through generations. For example, the area where the Marked Monster was attacked by Lewis and Chief Onongahkan—and where all the blood was found after Imogen disappeared—earned a nickname. Settlers called it the Sacred Square. You can see here, on this old map, where it was. Lewis forbade anyone to use it for any purpose. Curiously, it was reported that nothing grew there, even many years after the earth had been soaked with blood. Of course, that wouldn't have surprised the Q'ippicut; they always maintained that every part of the Keuhkkituh was poison.

"There was even a rumor that Imogen herself kept a diary . . . but it was never found. As the decades passed, sightings of the Marked Monster became far less common, you know. There have been no reports of anyone seeing it for nearly fifty years."

Just then a librarian poked her head into the archives room. "Mr. Carson? The copier's jammed. Would you mind taking a look?"

"I'll be back," Mr. Carson told Jenna as he eased himself off the chair. "And I'll copy some materials you can use in your research."

"Thank you," she said gratefully, her mind still whirling as she tried to process what the archivist had told her.

As soon as he was out of the room, she remembered something—the soft *thud* she'd heard inside Manfred

Lewis's desk when the lid banged down. With a quick glance toward the door, Jenna hurried back to the desk.

The lid still wouldn't open more than two inches, but it was wide enough for her to slip her hand inside. She wiggled her fingers around, trying to find . . .

Well. She wasn't sure what, exactly, she might find. But she wanted to know what was in the desk; *what* had fallen and made that noise.

Then Jenna's fingers brushed against something solid—something that inched across the wooden panel when she pushed it. It was smooth, small, and rectangular in shape; she could tell without even looking.

Slowly, carefully, she pulled her hand out of the desk and discovered that she was holding a small journal.

Jenna opened the book. On the first brown-spotted page she found an inscription that made her heart pound so hard she could hear it in her ears. But before she could read another word, she heard the *clump* of Mr. Carson's cane clunking across the floor.

He was on his way back to the archives room.

Jenna didn't even think. She acted entirely on instinct as she hid the journal in her notebook and fitted them into her backpack.

CHAPTER 7

Many hours later, pecking away at the keyboard while the rest of her family watched TV across the room, Jenna stretched and yawned. It felt fake to her—sounded fake, even—but must have been convincing enough, since Dr. Walker glanced at the clock on the DVD player and said, "It's getting late, Jenna. Will you be able to finish in fifteen minutes?"

Jenna knew she had to argue—at least a little—to be convincing. "Mom, it's not even nine o'clock!"

Dr. Walker sighed. "Yes. And fifteen more minutes on the computer, fifteen minutes getting ready for bed, fifteen minutes figuring out what you're going to wear tomorrow—it will be past nine thirty before you know it. Let's not have this argument again, please."

"Fine," Jenna said.

But secretly, she smiled to herself.

Never before in her life had Jenna rushed off to bed as quickly as she did that night. Alone at last in the solitude of her bedroom, she turned off all the lights and crawled into bed with a flashlight and the mysterious journal she'd smuggled out of the library.

It was just as she'd remembered.

The smooth grain of the leather cover.

The tear ripped across it.

Those suspicious, sickening splatters across the first page.

And, of course, the inscription:

THE DIARY OF IMOGEN LEWIS

AGED 15 YEARS, 4 MONTHS

IN THE YEAR OF OUR LORD 1767

Jenna's excitement at finding the diary of Imogen Lewis—from the very year in which Lewisville was founded; from the very year in which Imogen herself had disappeared—wasn't strong enough to overshadow her creeping sense of guilt. She could still hardly believe that she'd just *taken* the book like that. She had never done anything like that before in her life, and the more she thought about it, the worse she felt. *It's a library,* she told herself. *The whole point of that entire building is for people to borrow books. That's all I did—borrow a book. And I'll bring it back as soon as I'm done with it.*

But in her heart, Jenna knew that she was just making excuses. She hadn't borrowed the diary. She'd stolen it. And promising to bring it back didn't change the fact that she didn't have the right to take it in the first place. So she quickly pushed the thought from her mind, because she was obsessed with finding out whatever secrets Imogen might have recorded in her diary.

Jenna scrunched down under the covers and turned the page.

June 1, 1767

We have arrived at our new home! My eyes filled with tears of joy today as Papa planted the flag and announced in a most solemn voice: "I hereby proclaim these lands incorporated as the Town of Lewisville, and by the blessing of God may we prosper here as is only fitting for a people dedicated to hard work and the Holy Word as it is writ in the Bible." But I must be honest in this diary, if nowhere else, and confess that my tears were also for Mother and James and Mary and little Teddy. Never did I dream that they would not be standing with us on this day, and though Papa never speaks of them, never, I could tell he felt their absence as keenly as I did. When we first set out for

Jenna started flipping the pages. Not that she wasn't *interested* in the earliest days of Lewisville's founding . . . but a pressing sense of urgency forced her to skip ahead. In the middle of the diary, she came to several blank pages, and her heart sank.

Had Imogen stopped writing in her diary before the attack?

Some force compelled Jenna to keep turning the blank pages, and then, nearly three-quarters of the way through the journal, she found another entry, written in a shaky, unstable script.

August 30, 1767
With good reason I have abandoned my diary for more than a fortnight now, and I have left the

preceding pages blank so that I might, at some later date, record all that has happened in greater detail. For now, an abbreviated account must suffice. It pains me to commit these words to paper. I am unwell and advised not to exert myself. But if I do not write it, who will understand what has happened, when Papa has forbidden me to speak of it?

I erred grievously when I set off to pick wild blackberries in the woods. I thought I would make a pudding for Papa, as a surprise, but I should never have gone into the woods. I was warned. We all were. I should never have gone!

My ramblings took me off the path, through the thicket, and I was so preoccupied by the plump sweet berries that I——stupid!——did not realize how close I was to the forbidden Square, and I was not even quiet, but hummed to myself, and surely alerted the creature to my presence. I must have lost all track of the hour as I suddenly realized it was later than I expected, and night was fast approaching.

I heard the scratching first, and stopped, fearing a bear.

I wish it had just been a bear, for well-fed bears

are fat and lazy by the time the hottest days of August arrive, sated on all the bounty of the forest. A bear would not have troubled me so.

A chill of fear gripped my body and I stopped my humming, gathered my shawl around my shoulders, and made haste to return to the settlement. I know now that my fate was already sealed, and at that moment the creature was already watching me from the shadows.

The blow was so swift and so unexpected that I was knocked quite senseless and found myself sprawled on my back, most undignified, staring up through the gloomy pines at a darkening sky. My head was bleeding; I could feel the hot, sticky blood oozing over my left eye. Oh, WHY had I strayed from the path?

Then it appeared over me, the Beast, and so frightful that I cannot bear to write of it. It lifted one of its stumpy arms so that the claw, oh, the fearsome claws, glinted in the moonlight, sharp like knives, and one of them cut through my leg with such searing pain that I could not even cry out. I knew then that it would kill me and eat me.

I knew then that all hope was lost.

But I was wrong, thank God in Heaven, for the creature just sat back and stared at me as I writhed in pain. It lowered its horrible face and drank of the blood flowing from my wound. Then it stared into my eyes. Its own eyes glittered with a level of intelligence that I had never before seen in a beast.

To my surprise, it rose on its back legs and let out such a horrifying sound—a cry or a shriek or a growl or some combination of the three—that my heart nearly stopped from fear. Then it lumbered deeper into the woods, leaving me alone in the clearing.

Of course I tried to crawl back to the path, but I was too weak, and the pain in my leg was so great that I was sick, and I lay in the dirt and waited to die.

Some many hours later, when the August sun was beating down on me at the height of its brutality, I heard dear Papa's voice calling my name, and somehow found the strength to call back to him, and then his strong arms wrapped me up and lifted me into the air, and I must have passed out from the pain again, for when I awoke I was in my bed, safe,

and Mrs. Smythe was pressing a damp cloth to my
fevered face.

I am too weak and tired to write more tonight.

September 19, 1767

I am not myself.

The wound festers despite the many poultices
that Mrs. Smythe brings me each morning. I have
packed it with a hot mash of mustard and chamomile
and garlic—how it burns!—and still the wound does
not cease throbbing, red streaks like fire racing down
my leg. Papa doesn't say it, but I can see it in his
eyes: He fears I shall lose my leg.

October 13, 1767

Papa does not know that I heard his argument
with Chief Onongahkan tonight. Oh, I am gripped
with fear. The chief said that I have been Marked!
Marked for Death! That the wound will never heal.
That my blood thickens with a poison secreted
from the Monster's mouth. That the Monster hunts
for months in silent stealth and will draw me to
it, and if I resist its pull, it will come find me and

kill any who try to stand in its way.

Papa was so angry, but I could still hear the fear in his voice as he ordered the chief to leave us and never return. Oh, what shall I do?

What shall I do?

November 1, 1767

It waits for me.

I can hear it scratching, the scratching, the scratching. The scratching that never stops.

It calls for me in the darkest parts of the night when even the moon turns away from me, knowing that I cannot be saved. That I am not worth saving.

Oh, the Monster, out there in the night, waiting.

Its hunger grows, but it will wait. It will wait for me.

Oh God, can no one stop it?

Oh God, can no one save me?

November 9, 1767

This is no mere dream. This is no fevered hallucination. The creature calls me to him. The joy of the kill is prolonged in this way: that I know how I will die, and how it will hurt, and where it will happen, but not when.

What choice do I have in this matter? It knows where to find me. The stink of my rotting leg will guide it to me. There is nowhere for me to hide. There is no escape for me. My fate was sealed the moment I strayed from the path. I am

Jenna's heart thudded in her chest as she turned the page, but the entry ended abruptly. After that, Imogen's diary chronicled a descent into madness—undated fragments of writing so shaky that they were hard to read. Jenna pieced together phrases:

I want my mother.

Papa, I am sorry. Please forgive me.
I can be a Monster, I can cut. I am the poison in the wound.

I bleed. I never stop bleeding. What can soak up so much blood?

It draws me forth.

It is time.

Tonight.

It is better not to say good-bye.

I am choked with sobs and such bitter terror, yet already I feel freer knowing that the end is near.

It will all be over soon.

And that was all. Imogen hadn't written another word.

Jenna's hands were shaking as she closed the diary and put it on her bedside table. Then she changed her mind and carried it over to the bottom drawer of her dresser. She hid it there, where she usually stashed top secret notes from her friends, right next to the claw she'd found in the woods.

She crawled back into bed but knew it would be a long time before she'd fall asleep. She had so many questions. Why had the diary been hidden and locked away in the desk? What had happened to Imogen? Did the Marked Monster really mark her? Was her wound filled with a poison that made her go insane?

And the biggest question of all—what had really

happened to Imogen Lewis on the night she disappeared? Did the monster come for her, ripping the door off its hinges?

Or had Imogen, of her own free will, gone to it, and sacrificed herself to the monster's appetite?

Or had Imogen just gone crazy?

Jenna wasn't sure which was worse—asking those questions or knowing that they could never be answered. Yet as scared as she was, at some point she fell into a fitful sleep, filled with the kind of dreams that evaporate the moment you wake up.

She blinked in the darkness. *Why* was she awake?

Of course. Her arm. She must have rolled over onto it while she slept, and now it was throbbing painfully.

Jenna stumbled into the bathroom and rolled up her sleeve. She made a face of disgust when she saw the cut.

It was *much* worse, with a thin sheen of pus glistening over it. *Seriously, seriously, seriously gross,* Jenna thought as she rummaged through the medicine cabinet. When she poured hydrogen peroxide over the cut, it frothed and foamed. She grimaced in pain as she dabbed at it with a wad of toilet paper. Then she squirted half a tube of antibiotic ointment over the wound and covered it with a sterile bandage. *That ought to take care of it,* Jenna tried to reassure herself. The last thing she wanted to do was worry her parents. She was sure the cut would go away on its own, and her mother, the doctor was known to overreact.

But secretly, she wasn't so sure. Hadn't Imogen's diary chronicled the same thing—a wound from the Marked Monster that had not healed?

Well, Jenna told herself grimly, *I'll just have to wait and see. I'm sure it will get better with all that cream and stuff I put on it. I mean, it's got to be better than that frontier medicine Imogen had. Garlic in a cut? That's crazy.*

She went back into her bedroom, completely unprepared for what she saw in her bed.

The tip of a claw, peeking out from under her pillow.

CHAPTER 8

In the weak light coming from the hallway, the talon glinted ominously; winked, almost. Jenna immediately shut the door and turned on all the lights in her room. She had to be absolutely certain that she wasn't still asleep.

Wasn't still dreaming.

With a trembling hand, she reached out and forced herself to touch the claw. It was all too real, heavy and cold in her hand. She squeezed it, hard, trying to calm herself down.

There is a reasonable explanation for this, Jenna told herself, only a little surprised by how still she could sit when every muscle of her body was rigid with tension. *There is a reasonable explanation for why this claw is in my bed.*

Now all she had to do was figure out what it was.

Obviously the Marked Monster is not in my house, Jenna thought, starting with a statement of such undeniable fact that she was sure it would help her feel calmer. *Obviously that would be impossible. Obviously my entire family would wake up if there was a ten-foot monster stomping through my house, leaving its claw under my pillow.*

Still, just to make sure, she checked the bottom drawer of her dresser, and was immensely relieved to find Imogen's diary still there, but no claw. So the one in her hands was the same one she had found in the woods.

Jason, Jenna thought suddenly. *Maybe he—while I was in the bathroom—*

As swift and silent as a cat, she crept back into the hallway and paused right outside the door to her brother's bedroom. She held her breath as she creaked it open, half expecting Jason to jump out at her and scare her half to death. It wouldn't be the first time.

Her heart sank when she saw Jason sleeping peacefully in his bed. His chest rose and fell, rose and fell, keeping time with his deep, even breathing.

So it wasn't Jason, Jenna was forced to admit. *Jason isn't pranking me.*

That left one option.

I was sleepwalking, she thought. *Just sleepwalking, and whatever I was dreaming—or maybe from reading Imogen's diary—I got out of bed and got the claw. That's all.*

But the simplest, most practical explanation didn't make her feel any better. If anything, it made her feel worse. *What's wrong with me?* she wondered as she returned to her bedroom. *What's wrong with me? Why would I get up in the middle of the night and bring the claw into my bed?*

Jenna wrapped herself up in a quilt and curled up in the overstuffed armchair in the corner of her room. She couldn't answer any of those questions.

And she couldn't bear to sleep in her own bed, knowing that the claw had been cradled under her pillow, tainting the sheets.

On Tuesday, Jenna could think of just one thing: returning Imogen's diary to the library. Before school, she wrapped it in a towel and tucked it in the secret inner pocket of her backpack. All day long, in every class, she was distracted, thinking of the moment when the final bell would ring—and she could return the diary to the library, where it belonged. She didn't want to spend another minute with the thing.

At last the school day came to an end and Jenna bolted out the door and headed for the library.

Now all I have to do is get back into the archives room without Mr. Carson noticing me, and slip the diary back into the desk, she thought. *And then I can pretend like I never even found it.*

But despite the fact that school was out, the library was deserted; as Jenna walked inside, Mr. Carson looked up from the reference desk and waved at her. *Maybe I hurried here a little too quickly,* she thought ruefully.

"Hi, Mr. Carson," Jenna said as she approached the desk.

"Jenna! I'm glad to see you," Mr. Carson replied. "I found something that I think might be of great interest for your report."

"Really?" Jenna asked as she snuck a glance toward the archives room.

Mr. Carson must've noticed, though, because he started to chuckle. "Yes, yes! It's in the archives room. Come right this way," he said, and shuffled off.

Jenna followed him, hoping that she'd find an opportunity to slip the diary back into the desk. But Mr. Carson sat down and placed a piece of paper on the table.

"What's that?" Jenna asked with a mixture of curiosity and dread.

Mr. Carson didn't answer as he slid the paper over to her.

The long peace will end when you are least prepared,
When you have forsaken the Great Mother and the
ancient teachings.
You will not recognize the quiet;
The sign in the tree that slows the sap.
You will not understand that the sun-warmth
reaches the darkest places,
And as it warms the seeds, and coaxes forth the
shoots,
So, too, it wakes that which must not be woken.
Children of the Earth, mark these words.
Call forth the old memories, the ones most deeply
buried,
For that which is forgotten leads to the end of all.

Jenna read the poem twice before she looked up at the archivist. "What—what is this?"

"This is an old Q'ippicut poem," Mr. Carson explained. "I remembered it after we spoke yesterday and thought it might be useful for your project."

"But what does it mean?" Jenna asked.

"In the mid-1850s," Mr. Carson began, "long after Manfred Lewis and Chief Onongahkan had passed away, the residents of Lewisville began to talk about expanding the town's borders. One newcomer in particular had his eye on a tract of land that included the Sacred Square.

"The town council seemed poised to approve the expansion. But the new chief of the Q'ippicut interrupted their meeting and demanded that they honor the old promise. A heated argument broke out, and within two days' time, the Q'ippicut packed their belongings and set off for the Pacific Northwest. This poem is all that they left behind."

"They left?" Jenna asked. "Forever?"

Mr. Carson nodded. "And they never returned."

"Did the—did the settler build on the Sacred Square?"

"After all the fuss, no," Mr. Carson replied. "I suspect he was a little spooked by the legend and all the arguing. His property shared a border with the square, but it didn't encroach on it."

"So the fight was all for nothing," Jenna said. "The Q'ippicut left their home over nothing."

"Perhaps," Mr. Carson replied. "Or perhaps they were ready to leave. For many generations, the tribe had carried the responsibility of maintaining peace with the Marked Monster. I imagine that that was increasingly difficult as more European settlers arrived in the area."

"This poem doesn't say anything about the Marked Monster, though," Jenna pointed out.

"Yes, it does," Mr. Carson corrected her, pointing at the page. "This line here—'the sign in the tree that slows the sap.'"

"I don't understand."

"Didn't I mention that the other day? According to legend, the Keuhkkituh had long periods of hibernation. When it reemerged, it made its presence known by leaving one of its claws in a tree. The tree, of course, died after being pierced by the Keuhkkituh's claw. I suppose that whatever venom was in the claw would've poisoned the tree . . . Jenna? Jenna, are you all right?"

"What? Yes," she said quickly. "Why?"

"You look very pale," Mr. Carson replied. "Don't be afraid of these old legends and tales, my dear. I've lived in Lewisville for seventy-nine years and I've never seen the Keuhkkituh *or* its claw!"

Jenna didn't answer. As she read the poem again, Mr. Carson stood up. "The after-school rush will be here any minute," he said. "You can keep that copy of the poem, Jenna. I made it for you."

"Thanks," she said softly as Mr. Carson shuffled toward the door. Then she reached for her backpack.

"Jenna," Mr. Carson said in a voice so sharp it made her jump.

"What?" she asked anxiously.

Mr. Carson's eyes twinkled as he shook a finger. "Don't forget to wear gloves if you touch anything in here!"

"Of course," Jenna replied. "Thanks again."

As soon as he was gone, she unzipped her backpack; in a matter of seconds, she'd returned the diary to the dark recesses of Manfred Lewis's desk. *Back where it belongs,* she thought. Then she shoved the poem into her backpack and hurried out of the library, lost in thought.

Mr. Carson might not have seen the Keuhkkituh's claw before.

But Jenna had . . . stuck in a tree behind her house. She was certain of that now.

CHAPTER 9

After school on Wednesday, Maggie came over to Jenna's house so they could work on their posters for the big history project. Jenna was completely exhausted from staying up late the night before, writing the first draft of her paper. It didn't help that she wasn't sleeping well, either; her arm was still too sore for her to sleep on her left side, like she was used to. And every small sound in the night seemed to wake her; more than once Jenna had bolted upright in bed, her heart pounding furiously, all because she thought she heard something scratching at her window.

She never found the courage to check, though. Instead she crouched against the wall, with her blankets pulled up to her chin, watching the window and listening until at last she passed out from pure exhaustion.

"I'm so ready for summer vacation," Jenna said as she placed her poster board on the dining room table.

"Me too," replied Maggie. She dumped out a bag of construction paper, scissors, glue sticks, and double-sided tape. "Look at this. I think my mom bought out the art-supply store."

"This poster thing is so stupid," Jenna said, shaking her head. "Hello, we're in middle school! This is kindergarten stuff."

"No kidding," Maggie said. "I'm so bad at crafts. I can hardly draw a straight line."

"Looks like your mom thought of that," Jenna joked as she grabbed a ruler. Then she carefully started arranging her visual aids on the poster board: drawings of Manfred and Imogen Lewis; Manfred Lewis's sketch of the Marked Monster; the original map of Lewisville that Mr. Carson had showed her, with the Sacred Square marked in red; the Q'ippicut poem. And, of course, a bunch of captions she'd typed up on the computer the night before. Now they all had to be trimmed and matted on brightly colored pieces of card stock, then glued to the poster board. It was the kind of project that was going to take hours to complete, if Jenna wanted it to look good. The girls chatted quietly while they worked, occasionally helping each other with their posters.

After about an hour, they heard a key turn in the lock, and then the front door opened.

"Hi, Jenna, we're home!"

"Hi, Moron, we're home!"

"Jason, do not call your sister a moron," Mr. Walker said firmly.

"Hey, guys," Jenna said as her dad and brother walked in.

"Wow, what's going on here?" Mr. Walker asked as he walked over to the dining room and peered over Jenna's shoulder. "Working on the history project?"

"Yup," Jenna replied.

"Honey, that map is upside down," Mr. Walker pointed to the map Jenna had just glued down.

"Are you sure?" she asked with a frown.

"Definitely," Mr. Walker said.

"Argh!" Jenna groaned as she tried to peel the map off the poster board. Luckily, the glue was still damp, so she was able to remove the map without ripping it.

"What's this area marked in red?" Mr. Walker

asked. "Are you showing where you live?"

"No, that's the Sacred Square," Jenna replied. "It's where the chief of the Q'ippicut tribe attacked the Marked Monster in 1767."

"Huh," Mr. Walker said, nodding thoughtfully. "You know that's the clearing right behind our house, right? Jason, please go get the GPS out of my car."

"Make Jenna get it. It's her project."

"*Jason.*"

As Jason sighed loudly and dragged himself out to the car, Jenna squinted at her photocopy of the first map of Lewisville, which had been drawn by Manfred Lewis himself. It wasn't much of a map. Jenna could hardly recognize the area as the town where she'd lived for her entire life.

But when Jason brought back the GPS and her dad pulled up a map of modern-day Lewisville, Jenna realized that her father was right.

"See, it looks like this path became Briarcliff Road, and this one is definitely Arlington Avenue," Mr. Walker explained, tracing his finger along the map. "Our house was later built right around here—and our property borders the . . . what did you call it? The Sacred Square?"

Jenna nodded silently. She didn't trust herself to speak without everyone hearing the fear in her voice. There was no denying it now: The Sacred Square, where Manfred Lewis and Chief Onongahkan had attacked the Keuhkkituh, where Imogen Lewis had probably bled to death, was right behind the Walkers' backyard.

"Spooky!" Maggie said gleefully. "So the Sacred Square is where we're having our campout on Friday?"

"Oh, I almost forgot," Mr. Walker asked. "I'll go get the tent out of the basement and air it out. You don't want it smelling all musty for the first campout of the season."

As Mr. Walker went down the stairs to the basement, Jenna turned to Maggie. "Actually," she said slowly, "I've been thinking that we probably won't camp out. We can just have a sleepover in the house."

"What? No way!" Maggie exclaimed. "Why?"

Jenna shrugged. "I don't know. It's still kind of chilly at night," she said lamely.

"Don't be crazy. We all have warm sleeping bags," Maggie argued. "And everybody is so excited already. I know for a *fact* that Brittany already bought the stuff to make s'mores. She actually went a little overboard yesterday at—"

"I don't think Jenna's worried about the cold," Jason spoke up. "Look at her. She looks *scared*."

"I'm not scared," Jenna said hotly.

Jason knew right away that he'd hit a nerve. "Oh, you're not?" he cooed in a baby voice. "Itty bitty baby Jenna's not scared? Itty bitty baby Jenna's a big girl!"

"Come on, Jason," Maggie said. "Of course she's not scared. The campout was her idea. We're going to look for proof that the Marked Monster exists."

Maggie, stop talking. Maggie, stop talking, Jenna tried to psychically tell her friend. How could Maggie *not* know that she was giving Jason ammunition for his teasing?

"So *that's* it!" Jason exclaimed. "Baby Jenna's gotten all spooked about the Marked Monster since she started doing her research! Don't be scared, Jenna! I'm sure your little *friends* will protect you from the Big Bad Monster!"

"Shut up, Jason! You're such a jerk!" Jenna yelled at last—just as her dad came up from the basement, lugging the tent, tarp, and other camping supplies.

"Hey, watch it," he said with a frown. "You keep talking to your brother like that and you won't be having any sleepovers this weekend."

An awkward silence fell over the room. Maggie

stared down at her poster like she wished she could be invisible. Jenna could feel Jason smirking at her, but she refused to give him the satisfaction of looking his way.

"I'm going to start dinner," Mr. Walker continued.

Jenna stayed silent as she rotated the map and re-glued it to her poster.

"That's looking really good," Maggie said encouragingly. "You're definitely going to get a good grade on this!"

"Hope so," Jenna said quietly.

"Can you even *believe* that the Sacred Square is right behind your house?" Maggie asked. "Can I use your computer real quick? I want to e-mail Brit and Laurel to tell them! They are going to *freak out*. It's so creepy!"

"Uh, yeah. Sure."

As Maggie typed away, Jenna racked her brain, trying to think of a way—any way—to move the sleepover indoors. But how? Everybody loved campouts in the woods behind Jenna's house. The other girls were already psyched for the first campout of summer. And even if Jenna somehow did convince her friends to have a sleepover instead of a campout, Jason was just *waiting* for more reasons to make fun of her. He knew her better than she wanted to admit—and he was absolutely right about her fear. She could already tell that he'd tease her relentlessly about it. He'd never shut up about it.

Lost in thought, Jenna traced her finger around the area marked on the old map: the Sacred Square. Then she glanced out the window at the woods.

If Maggie and the others knew what had happened there—

That Manfred Lewis and Chief Onongahkan had attacked the Keuhkkituh and turned it into the Marked Monster—

That the monster's black blood had spilled there and that nothing, *nothing*, had grown from the polluted ground since—

That Imogen Lewis had probably bled to death on that very spot, a victim of the Marked Monster—

That almost two weeks ago, Jenna had found a claw in the tree—a sign from the Marked Monster announcing its return—

Jenna was certain they, too, would dread the thought of venturing into the Sacred Square, let alone spending an entire night there.

But how could she possibly tell them? It was all too crazy. They'd never believe it.

CHAPTER 10

Jenna had a burst of hope when she woke up on Friday morning, the day of the campout. She jumped out of bed and ran over to the window. But the minute she looked outside, her hopes were dashed. The sun was shining brightly in a beautiful blue sky. It was a gorgeous, late-spring day, practically perfect camping weather.

One rainstorm? she thought. *We couldn't have one big, soaking rainstorm to turn the Sacred Square into a mud pit?*

Now, Jenna knew, she was out of options. The campout was going to happen whether she wanted it to or not.

That was probably why her head was hurting so badly. Jenna rubbed at her temples and glanced long-ingly at her bed. All she wanted to do in that moment was crawl back into it, pull the blankets over her head, and sleep all day. Actually, now that she thought about it, it wasn't just her head that was hurting. Her whole body had started to ache—especially her left arm.

Jenna rolled up her sleeve and stared at the cut. It was looking more disgusting than ever, with red streaks radiating outward from the wound. *I'm going to have to wear long sleeves today,* she realized. *This cut is so gross.*

But, she tried to reassure herself, *at least it's not oozing anymore.* The thick, crusty scab had to be a sign that it was healing.

At least, that was what Jenna hoped.

After she got dressed, she went to the kitchen.

"Morning, sweet pea!" Dr. Walker said cheerfully. "Listen, Dad's got a meeting and won't be home until seven, and I'm going to be working tonight, so we won't be able to grill up hot dogs for the campout. I'm sorry. Do you want to order pizza instead?"

"Sure," Jenna said flatly. She grabbed a carton of blueberry yogurt out of the fridge and started to eat it at the counter. "Pizza's good. Whatever."

"Are you okay?" Dr. Walker asked, looking closely at Jenna's face.

"I have a headache," Jenna said, shrugging, still not

wanting to worry her mother about her arm.

"This warm weather," her mother said, shaking her head. "Allergy season is definitely here. Or do you think you're getting sick?"

"Sick? More like scared," Jason muttered under his breath.

Jenna rolled her eyes at him. "It's just allergies," she said.

"Honey, I'm putting some money on top of the fridge in case you want to order the pizza before Dad gets home from work," Dr. Walker said. "Have fun tonight! I'll see you in the morning!"

"Thanks, Mom," Jenna said, forcing a smile.

As the school day dragged on, Jenna felt worse and worse—not just from her pounding headache and achy muscles, but from the weight of dread that seemed to grow heavier with every passing hour. More than once, she wondered if she should just go to the nurse and try to get sent home from school. If she was sick she could skip the campout. But then a terrible thought struck her: *What if the rest of my friends go ahead with the campout?*

She shuddered to think of her friends, all alone in the Sacred Square, not knowing what she knew. They would be helpless against the Marked Monster if it showed up—and if anything happened to them, Jenna knew she could never forgive herself.

The house was empty when she got home from school; her friends wouldn't arrive for another two hours. *I'll just lie down for a minute and watch some TV,* Jenna decided as she stretched out on the overstuffed couch in the den. But before she could even turn on the TV, she fell asleep.

To feel so hot when everything is so cold; when the limbs of trees groan under the weight of ice and all the world glitters with snow. To face your doom with clear eyes. To walk, step by painful step, to your end. To know of the teeth and the talons. The breaking of bones. The tearing of flesh. And all your precious lifeblood will drain from your body. Your veins will empty and your skin will sink and your body will be nothing but a shell, and then your body will not be, and the earth will drink of your blood until all that's left of you is a dark stain in the dirt. You already know the last thing you will feel (pain); the last thing you will see (claws); and the last thing you will hear (a cry so sharp, so shrill)—

Jenna stirred just once before she sat bolt upright,

her heart pounding, her head throbbing, her ears splitting from the noise—

She stumbled off the couch and ran to the door before she realized that it was the phone and the doorbell, ringing simultaneously, that had jolted her from sleep. When she flung open the front door, she found Brittany and Laurel standing there.

"Finally!" Brittany said in a voice of supreme annoyance as she flipped her phone shut. Her auburn hair glinted in the late afternoon sun. "We've been ringing the doorbell for, like, ten minutes!"

"Sorry!" Jenna apologized as she held the door open for them. "I must've fallen asleep or something."

"Ooh, well played!" Laurel laughed. "You're really going to stay up all night, huh?"

"Yeah, well, we'll see," Jenna replied.

"Have you set up the tent?" asked Brittany.

"Not yet," Jenna admitted.

"Well, let's get out back and get started," Brittany declared. "Before the sun sets and it gets too dark to see anything out there."

"Is Maggie here?" Laurel asked.

"Uh, no," Jenna said. "She didn't come with you guys?"

Brittany and Laurel exchanged a look. "We, um, didn't call her, actually," Laurel admitted. "I assumed she would already be here."

"Oh. Well, I guess she'll be here soon," Jenna replied. "And if Jason and my dad aren't home by the time she gets here, she'll know where to find us, right?"

The girls made two trips to the clearing to carry their sleeping bags, backpacks, tent, and the stuffed grocery bag of snacks that Brittany had brought. The clearing wasn't far from the edge of Jenna's backyard—only about ten feet—but the dense trees completely blocked the house, making it seem like the girls had wandered much farther into the woods. A few bright rays of sunshine filtered through the tall pines surrounding the clearing. Though the sun wouldn't set for a couple of hours, the trees cast such long shadows through the clearing that it seemed like night was coming on fast. The girls worked quickly to pitch the tent, assembling it at the edge of the clearing near the base of the biggest pine—the same tree where Jenna had found the claw a couple of weeks ago. She could see that an amber vein of sap had crusted over the slit where the talon had been embedded. Jenna tried her hardest not to flinch at every little snapping twig or unusual sound she heard. *The woods are always full of weird noises,* she reminded herself.

Still, she wished that Brittany and Laurel would keep it down a little. They were making it so hard for her to really *listen* to the noises . . . just in case something was out there, lurking beyond the trees.

As the sun began to set, Jenna glanced around. "Where *is* Maggie?" she asked, glancing at her watch. "We said five o'clock, right? It's after six."

"I'll call her," Brittany offered, slipping her phone out of her pocket. Then she frowned. "I'm not getting any service, guys. Stupid trees."

There was a long silence.

"You don't think—" Laurel began.

"The Marked Monster?" Jenna cut her off. "I don't know! Do you think it was, like, waiting? What if she was walking out here all by herself and it *attacked* her?"

Brittany and Laurel stared at Jenna as if she'd lost her mind. "Um, I was going to say, you don't think she's waiting on your doorstep, really annoyed with us for not being at the house to let her in?" Laurel said slowly.

"Why would she sit on the doorstep for an hour?" Jenna asked crossly. "She knows we'd be in the clearing.

She'd at least come out here to check, right? I mean, she's not stupid!"

"Jenna, what's up with you?" Brittany asked. "You don't *actually* think Maggie got attacked by the Marked Monster, do you?"

Jenna opened her mouth and then closed it again quickly. The tone of Brittany's voice told her everything she needed to know: To the other girls, the Marked Monster was just a joke, a spooky story they told themselves to feel all freaked out. Jenna could still remember how fun that used to be.

If you only knew, she thought. *If you only knew what I know.*

But she didn't say anything like that. Instead she took a deep breath and said, "Let's go inside. We can see if Maggie's waiting out front. And we can call her."

She didn't mention the other reason why she wanted to go back: Any time spent away from the clearing, even just a few minutes, was a chance for her to feel safe. To *know* that she—and her friends—were out of the Marked Monster's reach.

When the girls got back to the house, there was no sign that Maggie had been there. Brittany called Maggie's house and let the phone ring for a long time . . . but no one answered.

Then, to Jenna's outrage, she found Jason sitting in front of the TV, chowing down on his fourth piece of pizza from the large box in front of him.

"Jason! Did you get that with the money Mom left me?" Jenna demanded as Brittany dialed Maggie's phone number again.

"Yeah. You're welcome," Jason said with that maddening smile. "I thought you'd appreciate it that dinner was waiting for you when you finished setting up the tent."

"That money was for *our* dinner," Jenna retorted. "Now you've eaten, like, *half* of it!"

"Oh yeah, you're right," Jason replied, trying to act surprised—and failing miserably. "My bad."

Jenna just shook her head and walked away. There would be plenty of time to make sure Jason got busted. For now, she had bigger things to worry about—like the disappearance of her best friend.

"I'm really worried," Jenna said anxiously. "Maggie is *never* late like this. She always calls. She's, like, superresponsible."

Brittany and Laurel didn't argue. "Jenna?" Brittany

asked. "When you were outside—and you talked about the Marked Monster—you seemed genuinely freaked out. Is—is that what's bothering you?"

"Ha! I knew it!" Jason crowed. "I knew you were scared!"

"Would you *shut up* already!" Jenna yelled. Then, to everyone's relief, the doorbell rang.

"Maggie!" Jenna cried out, forgetting to act cool. She raced to the door with Laurel and Brittany following right behind her. When she saw her best friend standing on the doorstep, she practically tackled her with a big hug.

"Whoa!" Maggie laughed. "What's up, Jenna? Sorry I'm late, everybody. My mom was driving me here from getting my braces tightened, but her car died and it took my dad *forever* to pick us up, and she didn't want me to walk the rest of the way because it was starting to get dark. You know how it is." As Maggie rolled her eyes, everyone laughed.

"I'm just glad you're okay," Jenna said quietly.

"Yeah, Jenna was really freaking out! She thought the Marked Monster was going to get you!" cracked Laurel.

"Oh, no doubt," Maggie said, nodding. "She's the expert on the Marked Monster, after all. Did she tell you guys about—"

"Wait, wait—tell us when we get back to the tent,"

Brittany interrupted her. "It'll be scarier that way."

"Is anybody else hungry?" Laurel asked.

"Doesn't matter if you're hungry or not," Jenna spoke up, trying to sound normal. "If you don't grab a slice, like, *now*, Jason will eat the whole pizza."

"We can't let that happen!" Brittany cried as she led the girls back to the living room. Amazingly, Jason had disappeared, leaving four slices in the box.

"I'm sorry, guys," Jenna said, shaking her head. "He's the worst."

"It's not a problem," Brittany replied. "I brought a ton of food. Don't worry about it."

Even though hours had passed since Jenna had eaten lunch, she found that she wasn't hungry at all. She picked at her slice of pizza, nibbling the crust so her friends wouldn't notice that she wasn't really eating. While they ate, the sun dipped below the trees, and darkness fell over the Sacred Square.

"All right," Maggie finally said as she wiped her greasy hands on a napkin, "let's get out there and look for the Marked Monster!"

"Okay," Jenna said, nodding as she tried to psych herself up. "Let's do this."

On the way back out to the clearing, she paused to get some food for the stray cat. She poured a large pile of it at the tree stump near the back of her yard.

"Kitty treats?" asked Laurel with a laugh. "Don't you think the Marked Monster will want, like, fresh meat instead?"

Jenna tried to join in her friends' laughter too. "This is for the stray cat," she explained. "Even though I haven't seen it all week. Besides, the Marked Monster doesn't exist, right?"

If I say it enough, maybe I will make it true, Jenna thought.

At this point, it was so dark that the girls could hardly see. "Did we leave our lanterns back at the tent?" Laurel asked. "That was really genius, wasn't it?"

"Come on," Maggie said, glancing at the sky, where the moon shone through a thin veil of clouds. "We can find our way. Just stick together." The girls grabbed hands and crashed through the underbrush on their way to the clearing, laughing and shrieking.

"Shh, shh, shh!" Jenna hissed. "Do you guys have to make so much noise? Seriously. *Shhhhh!*"

An awkward silence fell over the girls as they reached the tent. One by one, they climbed inside, and Brittany switched on her lantern. Then she turned to Jenna.

"What is your problem?" Brittany asked. Her scowling face was ghostly in the long shadows from the lantern. "You are no fun tonight."

"Whatever."

"No, I mean it," Brittany said. "Do you want us to go or something?"

"No," Jenna replied. "I just don't know why you have to make so much noise."

"Actually, Jenna, is everything okay?" Maggie asked gently. "You seem, like, really stressed."

"*Really* stressed," Laurel added.

"I'm fine," Jenna said firmly. "It's just—if you guys keep making so much noise, you might scare it away. And then we won't get any proof." She hoped that her small lie would keep them from figuring out why she really wanted them to be quiet—so that they wouldn't actually draw the monster to them.

"Right." Brittany laughed. "I'm so sure the Marked Monster would be afraid of *us*. Now look," she continued as she dug through her backpack. "My cell phone has a video camera, and I snuck this out of my dad's stuff."

Jenna watched as Brittany revealed a heavy, expensive-looking camera with a special flash on top of it.

"Ever since my dad got into photography, he's been buying all kinds of fancy camera gear," Brittany said importantly. "So I, you know, borrowed some of his stuff, like this low-light lens and special flash system that take pictures in the dark."

"Wouldn't you get busted if your dad knew you took that?" Laurel asked, her eyes wide.

"Well, who's going to tell him?" Brittany asked. "As long as it doesn't get broken or anything, we should—"

"Shhhh!"

All eyes turned to Jenna, who was holding up one hand. Her head was tilted to the side as if she was straining to hear something.

Brittany sighed loudly. "*Again* with the shushing? I swear to God, you're worse than—"

"*For one minute would you shut up?*" Jenna said in a voice so cold that even Brittany stopped talking.

The girls sat in silence for a moment.

Then everyone else heard it too:

Drip.

Another silence.

Drip.

Even in the low beam of the flashlight, it was

impossible to miss the tension etched on Jenna's face.

"It, you know, it was getting cloudy," Laurel whispered. "Maybe that's just a, you know, raindrop or something."

Drip.

"The tent's waterproof," Maggie offered, also in a whisper.

But nothing could change the look on Jenna's face. Slowly she reached across the tent for Brittany's flashlight, without saying a word.

Drip.

The girls watched as Jenna pointed the flashlight up to the top of the tent.

Drip.

Even through the nylon of the tent, everyone could see the viscous liquid falling in single drops and oozing down the side of the tent in a single gory stream.

Drip.

Too thick to be water.

Drip.

Too dark to be rain.

Drip.

CHAPTER 11

"What is—is that—what is that, blood?" Laurel asked haltingly. "What *is* that?"

Drip.

Jenna immediately turned off the lantern.

"Turn it on!" Brittany said. "Turn it on!"

"No," Jenna whispered. "Whatever is out there—we don't want it to see the light. We don't want it to see *us*."

Drip.

"Jenna, *why* is there blood falling on your tent?" Maggie asked. Her voice was high and tight, straining against hysteria. "We should—I want—we should—"

"Go inside," Jenna finished for her. "We have to get into the house. But we have to be smart about this. We have to be—careful. Just—for a minute—*listen*."

Drip.

Drip.

Drip.

With every drop that fell on the tent, Jenna's stomach lurched; if she'd eaten more pizza she would've thrown up for sure. But, as sickening as the drops were, they were all she could hear: no rustling in the bushes, no crackling of twigs. And, perhaps most hopeful of all— no scratching.

Drip.

"Okay," Jenna finally whispered. "When I count to three, we'll all—*slowly*—get out of the tent and—*slowly*— walk back to the house. As quietly as"—*Drip*—"we can. Understand?"

"Yes," chorused the other girls in a whisper.

Drip.

"One. Two. Three."

Slowly, and as silently as possible, Jenna unzipped the mesh door of the tent. One by one, her friends slipped out into the darkness, until Jenna was the only one left.

Drip.

But when it came time for Jenna to venture into the night, she lost the will to leave.

Go, she told herself. *Go. It's not safe here. This tent can't protect you. So go. Go.*

Somehow she found the courage to step out of the tent. And then, suddenly, she had the urge to turn on the lantern. To take a closer look at the blood.

She didn't fight it.

The beam of the light cut through the darkness. Jenna stepped toward the side of the tent, where the blood was now flowing in several streams.

"Jenna!" one of her friends called from the woods. "What are you doing?"

She didn't answer. She squinted her eyes as she peered at the tent and gave thanks that it was too dark for her friends to see her reach out and touch the blood. It glistened red and sticky on her finger.

She would never quite understand what compelled her to do what she did next.

Jenna raised her finger to her nose and smelled it.

For the briefest instant, she frowned in confusion. The liquid on her finger didn't smell metallic like blood. It smelled . . . sweet. Suddenly she started to laugh. "This isn't blood," she called to her friends. "It's syrup. With, like, food coloring in it. *Jason!* Where are you, you loser? I know what you did, Jason! I know what you did!"

Jenna swung the lantern around wildly, trying to spot her brother hiding in the bushes or behind a tree. There was no way Jason would miss this moment, she knew. No way.

It didn't take her long to find him, crouched on a tree branch right above the tent, holding a sports bottle filled with the gory liquid. He was red-faced and shaking with silent laughter. As he jumped down from the tree, Jenna was so angry she was about to scream, but Jason started talking first.

"My sister, brave enough to touch blood!" he yelled, holding up his hand for a high five. "Jenna, that was hard-core. I didn't know you had it in you! I have to say I'm impressed."

As he doubled over with laughter, the other girls came back to the tent, wearing goofy grins of relief.

"What is your *problem*, Jason?" Jenna exploded. "What's the matter, you don't have any friends of your own? This is your idea of a fun Friday night, trying to scare me and *my* friends?"

"Oh, there was no *trying* about it," Jason said, still laughing. "I wish I had a video camera so you could see how terrified you guys were, crawling out of the tent like the Marked Monster was about to swoop down and *eat* you or something!"

One by one, the other girls started to laugh—except for Jenna.

"Come on, Jenna, you have to admit that was an awesome prank," Brittany said. "Right?"

"Thank you," Jason said, holding up his hand to high-five Brittany—and accidentally brushing against Jenna's left arm. She gasped in pain and reflexively turned away, trying to hold her injured arm close.

"Give it a rest, Jenna," Jason said in annoyance. "I barely touched you! And Mom isn't here, so your over-reacting isn't going to get me in trouble this time."

Jenna didn't respond.

"Thank God that wasn't real blood, right?" Maggie asked. "That would've been *sick*."

"You guys really thought that was funny?" Jenna asked her friends. "You weren't laughing when we were in the tent."

"Oh, lighten up!" Brittany said, making a face. Then she turned to Jason. "She's been in this bad mood all evening. Don't worry about her. *I* thought it was hilarious."

Jason stopped laughing and looked closely at Jenna. "Are you okay?"

"Yeah. I'm fine," she said, pushing her blond hair behind her ears. "What's wrong?"

Jason shook his head. "That's what I'm asking you. You seem . . . weird."

"I'm *fine*," Jenna said, more forcefully than she meant. "Honestly, *you're* the weird one, hanging out in a tree with a bottle of fake blood."

Everyone laughed again, but Jason continued to look at Jenna in a way that unsettled her. She tossed her head defiantly as she marched back to the tent and ducked inside.

There, away from her friends and her brother, she pressed her cold hands to her face. Her cheeks were burning. She didn't know if it was the stress of Jason's prank, or just the aftereffects of a sleepless week, but Jenna had never felt sicker in her life, except for that time in fifth grade when she'd had the flu. *What is wrong with me?* she asked as she rubbed her temples.

Not even in the secret-most place of her mind could Jenna admit it, but in her heart, she couldn't shake the fear that she was poisoned like Imogen Lewis. She could almost feel the venom of the Marked Monster pumping through her veins, slipping into her cells, making her sick, making her crazy.

Stupid, she told herself, shaking her head. *Shut up.*

"Jenna? Are you *talking* to yourself?" Jason asked, poking his head into the tent.

I was talking? Jenna wondered. *Aloud?*

"No," she shot back. "I was talking to you."

Jason pushed his way into the tent, followed by Jenna's friends. His eyes never left her face.

"Seriously, *go*," Jenna said to him. "Leave us alone."

"Actually, I kind of want to stay," Jason replied. "Who knows—could get interesting, if the Marked Monster shows up."

"Well, we *don't* want you to stay," Jenna began.

Brittany cut her off. "It's cool with me, Jenna."

"Yeah, I don't mind," Laurel spoke up. "For a little while, anyway."

As Jenna's best friend, Maggie knew better than to say anything. Jenna just shook her head in frustration as Jason picked up Brittany's dad's camera.

"Wow, this is sweet," he said. "Where did you get this?"

"It's my dad's," Brittany said, smiling at Jason in a

way that made her look ridiculous. "Want to try it out?"

"Can I?" he asked eagerly.

As Brittany showed Jason how to adjust the settings on the camera, Maggie caught Jenna's eye and made a face like she was blowing kisses. Jenna responded by pretending to stick her finger down her throat. It wasn't exactly a secret that Brittany had a little crush on Jason, but she wasn't usually so obvious about it.

Suddenly Jenna heard it: the scratching. Almost a whole day had passed without her hearing that terrible noise, but now it was back. A chill of fear rippled over her skin, and she shivered.

"Shhhhh!" she whispered loudly, holding up one hand.

At the wild, feverish look in her eyes, everyone obeyed.

"You hear that, right?" Jenna asked hoarsely. "You hear it? The scratching?"

Desperately she looked from face to face, but all she saw were blank stares.

"I'm not crazy, I'm not, I'm not," Jenna babbled. "Just listen. Listen. You'll hear it, you *have* to hear it—"

"Jenna, quiet," Jason said suddenly.

Jenna held her breath, hardly daring to hope—

"I heard something," he said.

Please, Jason, don't make fun of me, Jenna thought. *Not now. Not about this.*

"Me too," Brittany spoke up.

"Scratching?" Jenna asked.

Jason shook his head. "No, like rustling. Like there's something—something in the bushes."

"Was it—" Laurel began at the same time as Maggie said, "I didn't hear—"

"Everybody shut up," Jason ordered. "I want to listen."

In the silence, in the tent, in the middle of the Sacred Square, the darkness had physical qualities that seemed new and strange to Jenna. It was heavy; it was pushing her down, down, or the earth was rising up to swallow her. She grasped the edges of her sleeping bag so that she could have something to hold on to.

When the rustling came again, there was no question that everyone heard it. And there was no question that there was something in the bushes—something alive.

Suddenly the entire tent shuddered, as if some unseen force had rushed into it, had tried to rip it from the stakes that held it to the ground. The nylon flaps shuddered and were still.

"What was that?" Jason asked sharply.

The fear rising in Jenna made her dizzy. This was no prank; this was no pesky brother; this was something alive, something sinister, just outside the tent; something that had run out of patience; that would wait not a moment longer to claim its due—

Jenna's cry broke the silence. "It's here. It's here. The Marked Monster. It's come for me."

Her fear spread quicker than fire. It filled the tent like smoke until the other girls were choked with it.

"Jenna, keep it together," Jason snapped. "There's no such thing as the Marked Monster, okay?"

Jenna wrapped her arms around her knees and rocked back and forth, back and forth. If he knew—if *only* he knew—

Well, she realized. *I can show him*. Then *he'll know*.

Jenna grabbed a huge flashlight—a heavy-duty industrial one that belonged to Maggie's dad, a plumber—and crept over to the entrance to the tent. "Jason," she croaked, "come over here. Come see."

Jason was at her side in an instant.

"Don't do it, Jenna, don't open the tent!" Maggie begged.

Jenna and Jason exchanged a glance, and Jenna knew that they were in complete agreement. Whatever was out there, they were going to see it. "I'll open the flap, you hold the light," Jason whispered. "And I'll try to take a picture. Okay?"

Jenna nodded. This was it.

The metal teeth of the zipper made an agonizing ripping sound as Jason tried to unzip the tent as quietly as possible. When the door flapped open and Jason, crouching low, held up the camera, Jenna knew it was time.

She pushed the rubber button on the flashlight and swung a blinding beam into the darkness just outside the tent. It was hard to see what exactly stood there, just feet from the tent—but the eyes, oh, the eyes. . . . If she survived this night, Jenna knew that she would never forget those eyes, red and glittery in the darkness, hovering ten feet above the ground.

CHAPTER 12

The camera flashed, the . . . thing . . . howled, and Jenna, in her fear, dropped the flashlight. There was another thundering rustle through the bushes. By the time Jenna scrambled to pick up the flashlight, the . . . thing . . . was gone.

Jason yanked his sister back into the tent and zipped the door closed. His face was paler than she'd ever seen it before.

"You saw it?" Jenna whispered. "You saw the Marked Monster?"

He looked away. "I saw something. I don't *know* it was the Marked Monster. It was *something*."

"Then what was it?" Jenna asked him.

He shrugged. "Maybe it was a squirrel?"

"Too big."

"A raccoon?"

"Do raccoons even climb trees?" Jenna shot back.

"Yes! Don't they?"

"How would I know what raccoons do? Do I look like someone who knows *anything* about raccoons?"

"Guys?" Laurel spoke up tentatively. "Did you get a picture?"

Jason started scrolling through the camera. "I tried," he said. "Let me see . . . yeah . . . it's, well, this—"

The girls crowded around the camera's tiny digital screen. Jason had managed to snap a picture, but it only showed the animal's eyes. There was a soullessness in them; a hungry emptiness in those eyes that struck the heart with fear.

One thing was certain: That was no squirrel. But the picture was so dark, there was no way to tell what it really was.

"I, uh, I don't want to camp out anymore," Brittany said bluntly. "You were right, Jenna. This is too freaky. I'm going in."

"Me too," Laurel chimed in.

But Jenna shook her head. "I have to see this

130

through," she said. "If that's the Marked Monster, I have to get proof. Real proof. I have to *know*."

"I'll stay," Jason told her. "I'll see it through with you."

"So will I," added Maggie.

For a moment, Brittany looked like she regretted her announcement that she was going back to the house. Then she stood up and said, "Well, we shouldn't split up. That's just stupid."

"I'm not going in," Jenna said stubbornly. "Not until we know what's out there."

"I can't stay out here!" Laurel cried suddenly. "What's *wrong* with you guys? Things are really, really freaky. It's not safe out here!"

Maggie held up her hands. "Look. Let's not over-react," she said. "Jason's probably right that it was just a raccoon or something. Or a possum. So Laurel and Brittany, if you guys want to go back to the house, you should. We'll be there soon."

"Come on, Laurel," Brittany said after a long silence. "Good luck, you guys. Don't stay out here long. Seriously—don't do anything stupid."

"Be careful," Jenna whispered as Brittany and Laurel stepped out of the tent into the night.

Then they were gone.

"So," Maggie said, her voice shaky, "what do we do now?"

"We get ready," Jenna replied. She turned to her brother. "Jason—the camera—can you set it up better? So we can take a better picture?"

"I, uh, I think so," Jason said as he fiddled with the camera's settings. "I mean, I'll do my best."

"And when that's ready, we wait," Jenna replied.

"For what?" asked Maggie.

"For the Marked Monster to return."

"But Jenna," Maggie said, "how do you know it will come back?"

Jenna shut her eyes; saw those hungry, empty eyes; heard the scratching. Always, the scratching. "It will."

They waited in tortured silence for five minutes, ten, fifteen.

But nothing happened.

"That thing knows we're here," Jason finally said. "I don't know why it hasn't come back. Unless we scared it—with the light—and the noise—"

"It's not afraid," Jenna said. "It is *not* afraid. Not of us."

"Maybe you should call it," Maggie suggested.

Jenna and Jason turned to her with questions in their eyes.

"You know," Maggie continued. "Like at the sleepover last week. That noise you made—when you told that story. You know."

Slowly Jenna started to nod. "Yeah," she said. "I could call it. We could get ready to take a picture and I could call it here. And then we could—we would—"

"We would know," Jason finished for her.

Nothing more needed to be said. They stepped out of the tent into the silent clearing. Wispy clouds scuttled across the moon, casting eerie shadows that filled the Sacred Square with moving patches of light, as if the shadows themselves had come to life and started creeping across the ground. Jenna watched her brother fiddle with the camera's settings one last time. She felt an odd detachment from the people around her, as if she were preparing herself to say good-bye.

"Ready?" she asked.

"Ready," he replied.

Jenna steadied herself and made the call:

"Aiiiii-ck-ck-ck-ck!"

Again:

"Aiiiii-ck-ck-ck-ck!"

Silence.

They waited.

The silence—*Too quiet,* Jenna thought, *too quiet in these woods; no sounds, no noise, nothing, it's too quiet*—stretched all around them.

A tentative smile flitted across her lips. "Maybe it *was* a raccoon," she whispered. "In the trees."

"Call again," Jason encouraged her.

"Yeah, just one more time," Maggie replied. "And then we'll go in. We'll know. As much as we ever could, anyway."

Jenna nodded, though her throat was dry and raspy from making that awful sound. She took a deep breath and made, for the last time in her life, the call:

"Aiiiii-ck-ck-ck!"

That was it. They'd gone into the woods and they'd tried to find the Marked Monster. They'd failed. And that was okay. Jenna smiled in the darkness, knowing that this would turn into a story she and her friends would tell for years, tell until it lost all the fear and became funny. She could see it so clearly, the four of them sitting up late at night, howling with laughter until their sides ached.

"Aiiiii-ck-ck-ck-ck!"

The sound shattered the night. Maggie and Jason spun around to look at Jenna.

"That wasn't me," she said. "That time it wasn't me!"

The cry, throaty and garbled, came again, so shrill that it made Jenna's ears ache. She clapped her hands over them and wished, for one brief moment, that this was all a dream, nothing more than a terrible nightmare from which she would awake sweaty and scared but ultimately safe.

This was no nightmare, though. This night was all too real. And just when Jenna thought things couldn't get worse, the sound of footsteps thundering through the brush echoed through the Sacred Square.

The Marked Monster was approaching.

Quickly.

"Run!" Jenna screamed at the top of her lungs. "Run!"

Maggie and Jason took off for the house, with Jenna right behind them. No matter how fast she ran, she felt that the monster was moving faster, bearing down on them, and a horrible, foul stench filled her nostrils—the sweet stink of death, of flesh rotting away into nothingness, so close she could almost taste decay on her tongue.

Then, just ahead, she saw her house, glowing with

warm lights, and Brittany and Laurel holding open the door, identical expressions of fear on their faces.

"Hurry! Hurry!" Brittany was yelling. And they did, first Maggie, then Jason, and now it was Jenna's turn, and the door was held wide open for her. She was almost home.

She stopped. Turned to face the forest.

It was waiting for her there, just beyond the trees.

It would wait for her. If not tonight, then tomorrow night, or the next. Jenna was sure of it. Unless she met it face-to-face, and scared it off, she would never be free of it . . . or of her fear. *I am one of the Marked,* she thought. *I am marked by the Monster.*

What weapon did Jenna have to use against the Marked Monster? How could she ever frighten it away?

I have the light, she thought, feeling the weight of the industrial flashlight, heavier than she remembered. *I have the light.*

And if that didn't work?

Jenna remembered the words from Imogen's diary: "Already I feel freer knowing that the end is near. It will all be over soon."

"Jenna," Jason said. His voice sounded hollow, far

away; like he was standing at the end of a long tunnel. "Jenna, get inside."

But the pull was too strong for her to fight.

It is better not to say good-bye.

"I'm sorry," Jenna whispered.

Then she turned around and bolted, disappearing into the darkest depths of the woods.

"Jenna!" Jason yelled after her. He started to run out the door, but Brittany grabbed his arm and wouldn't let go.

"You can't go back!" she babbled. "You can't go back!"

In strained silence, they watched the beam of Jenna's flashlight bobbing among the trees. Then a thud, a sudden darkness, and one last, terrible sound: Jenna's scream, echoing through the night.

CHAPTER 13

"I don't understand how this happened," Mr. Walker said, running his fingers through his sparse hair so that it stood up wildly. "How did this happen, Jason?"

"I don't know," Jason mumbled, looking at the ground.

"That's not good enough!" snapped Mr. Walker. "She's your little sister, Jason! You're supposed to look out for her!"

"I tried!" Jason exploded. "Why do you think I stayed with her in the woods? At her stupid campout! I could tell something was wrong with her. I *asked* her. But she wouldn't tell me anything."

Mr. Walker sighed and sat down heavily. "I'm sorry, Jas," he said. "It's late. I know we're both anxious."

Jason nodded without saying a word. It had been more than two hours since they'd found Jenna, unconscious and unresponsive, in the clearing, and nearly an hour since the other girls at the campout had gone home with their parents and Dr. Walker had rushed home from the hospital and started treating Jenna's arm. Jason would never forget the look on his mother's face when she first saw it. That look—the momentary lapse in her normally calm demeanor—had scared him worse than Jenna's injuries, with the angry red streaks racing down her arm and the foul green liquid flowing from it.

And now this long, long stretch, with Mom and Jenna locked away in the bathroom, and Jenna's friends all gone home, and just Jason and Mr. Walker to wait, in the quiet; to wait, with the worry.

"How much longer?" Jason finally asked. "This is taking kind of a long time, isn't it?"

Mr. Walker sighed. "Maybe we should have gone to the hospital."

Just then Dr. Walker's voice echoed down the hall. "Carl? Jason? Can you help me move her back to her bedroom? I'm done in here."

Like a flash, Mr. Walker and Jason were at the

bathroom, where they found Jenna slumped against the cold tile of the bathtub. Her face was very pale, almost gray.

"Is she going to be okay?" Mr. Walker said right away as he knelt by Jenna's side.

Dr. Walker paused before she answered. "We'll need to watch that wound very closely tomorrow," she finally replied. "I gave her an antibiotic shot, but if it gets any worse, I'm taking her to the hospital. I don't want her to . . ."

As her voice trailed off, Dr. Walker and Mr. Walker exchanged a glance.

"What?" asked Jason. "You don't want her to what?"

"To lose her arm," Dr. Walker answered. "But that's not going to happen, honey. If the antibiotics don't kick in by tomorrow night, we'll take her to the hospital and start an IV."

From the floor, Jenna groaned.

"Let's get her into bed," Dr. Walker whispered. "Careful—try not to touch her arm."

As gently as they could, Jason and Mr. Walker picked her up. Jason tried not to look at the pile of bloody towels in the bathtub. At least the bandage on Jenna's arm was very clean and dry, bright white gauze gleaming under the bathroom lights.

Halfway down the hall to Jenna's room, her eyes fluttered open.

"Jenna?" Jason asked hopefully. "Are you okay?"

She shook her head, just a bit, before her eyes closed again, but the fact that she had responded at all, that she'd seemed to understand his question, filled Jason with hope.

Carefully Mr. Walker and Jason lay Jenna down on her bed. She didn't open her eyes again. In the doorway, Dr. Walker whispered, "I'm going to stay in here tonight. In case Jenna needs me."

"I don't know," Mr. Walker began. "Maybe we should take her to the hospital."

"If we need to, we will," Dr. Walker replied. Then she closed the door.

It was early afternoon before Jenna opened her eyes again, blinked, blinked once more. She had never realized before how comfortable her bed was; how cheerful her room, when the warm sunlight streamed through the gauzy curtains. She closed her eyes again, just to open them and feel the sweet, sweet relief of being in her ordinary bedroom.

Across the room, her mother dozed in a chair. Jenna hated to wake her, but—

Dr. Walker's eyes opened. "Hey there, sleepyhead. How are you feeling?"

"Um, okay?" Jenna said tentatively. "Tired. Sore."

Dr. Walker nodded. "That's to be expected. Can I get Dad and Jason? They've been dying to see you."

Jenna nodded. She was trying so hard to remember what had happened, but the memories of the night before were as sharp and irregular as shattered glass. Jenna had the sense that if only she could put the pieces back together, she would *understand*—she would *know*—

"Jenna!" Mr. Walker exclaimed as he hurried into the room. "Jenna, how are you feeling?"

"Hey," Jason said awkwardly from the doorway.

"Hey," Jenna replied. "What—what happened?"

"You don't remember?" Jason asked.

She shook her head.

"Honey, what happened to your arm?" Dr. Walker asked.

"It was so stupid, actually," Jenna said. "I found this claw thing in the woods, and we were messing around with it at Maggie's sleepover last weekend, and it accidentally scratched me. It was such a little cut, but it got really gross, even though I put, like, a ton of antibiotic ointment on it every day."

"You should have showed me those cuts, Jenna," Dr. Walker said gently. "They were really, really infected. You probably needed to start taking an antibiotic *days* ago."

"Cuts?" Jenna asked. "I only had one cut."

"No, honey, there were two cuts," Dr. Walker said. "I cleaned them out myself."

Jenna craned her neck and tried to peel up a corner of the gauze to see.

"Don't touch it," Dr. Walker told her. "Besides, after the debridement I did to clean the wounds, it's all one big sore now. You needed fifteen stitches!"

Jenna scrunched up her face. "*Yuck.* But I only had one cut, Mom. I know it."

"Maybe it happened while you were in the woods," Mr. Walker suggested. "Do you remember anything?"

Jenna's face clouded over. "I went out there to . . . find the Marked Monster," she said slowly. "And . . .

I dropped the light . . . and . . ."

"And then what?" Jason asked eagerly.

"I don't remember!" Jenna exclaimed. "Mom, why can't I remember?"

"Your fever was so high, sweetie," Dr. Walker said. "Dad and Jason found you passed out in the clearing— you were burning up—"

"But I have to remember!" Jenna said, her voice rising an octave. "I *have* to know!"

"Know what?" asked Dr. Walker.

"Nothing," Jenna said sullenly. She already knew how weird it would sound to tell everyone that she was convinced that the Marked Monster still lurked in the woods.

Suddenly she remembered: Jason. He had been there too. Across the room, their eyes met.

"I'm starving," Jenna said abruptly as she swung her legs over the side of the bed. "Do we have any food?"

"Whoa, take it easy, Jenna," Dr. Walker said. "I really want you to rest."

"I'm feeling . . . good, actually," Jenna said. "I think I can make it to the kitchen. And I'm really, *really* hungry."

"Well, that's good," Dr. Walker said. "Let's go."

Sitting at the kitchen table, Jenna ate three bowls of

pasta. Food had never tasted so delicious!

"Hey, Jason, how was your karate meet this morning?" Jenna remembered to ask.

"Oh. I, uh, skipped it actually. We were still waiting for you to wake up, so I thought I'd stick around." He stood up abruptly. "I'd better go get the tent and stuff. We left it in the clearing all night."

"I'll come with you," Jenna said right away.

"No, I want you to rest," argued Dr. Walker.

"Mom. I really feel a *lot* better," Jenna said.

Dr. Walker sighed. "Just for a couple of minutes, okay? And Jason, stay with her the whole time. I really don't want you to overdo it, Jenna. No heavy lifting, no exertion."

"I won't, Mom," Jenna promised.

On the way out, she brought the box of cat food . . . just in case. And, to her delight, the stray was waiting for her at the tree stump.

"Hey, little sweetie!" Jenna cried as the purring cat leaped onto the stump. "Where've you been all week?"

"Jenna, don't touch it," Jason said. "It could have rabies or something. Don't you have enough germs?"

Ordinarily, Jenna would have tried to come up with

some clever retort, but there was something protective in Jason's voice that made her hold back. "Well, Jason, I didn't know you cared."

"Yeah, well, you *are* my only sister," he replied. "I'd rather you not, like, *die* or anything."

"Me either," Jenna said, laughing genuinely for the first time in days.

It felt so good to laugh, in the sunshine, with Jason next to her. But the trees stood before them, tall and silent, casting long shadows over the yard.

"I, um, I actually owe you an apology," Jason began.

"What did you do this time?"

"That claw thing? In your room the other night? I was the one who put it in your bed when I heard you get up," Jason admitted. "To freak you out."

"I *thought* it was you!" Jenna exclaimed. "But you were sleeping when I peeked in your room."

"You *thought* I was sleeping," Jason corrected her. "Anyway—forgive me? I'm actually really sorry about that. It seemed funny at the time."

"You're forgiven," Jenna said with a sigh. "But how did you know where to find it?"

Jason gave her a funny smile. "I'm sure I'll regret

admitting this, but Jenna, let's just say you need to find a new secret hiding place. I've known about that one for years."

Jenna was about to start yelling at her brother for going through her stuff when she realized that even though Jason could've read all the notes from her friends, he'd never used them to embarrass her. *Maybe,* she thought, *he hadn't even read them.*

"Do *not* snoop through my room anymore," she said firmly. "And could you *try* not to be such a huge loser?"

"I'll see what I can do," Jason replied. Then he nodded toward the woods. "You sure you're up for this?"

"I think so," Jenna said. "I just . . . want to go back. For a minute, at least."

They walked into the woods without saying another word, passing through the golden sunlight that filtered through the trees. It was all so pretty and peaceful, so *calm,* even, that Jenna had trouble believing it was the same place she'd been so terrified the night before. *Maybe I let my imagination run away with me,* she thought. *Maybe Mom was right, and it was all because of the fever.*

"Here we are," Jason said quietly when they reached the clearing.

"Oh, man, what happened to the tent?" asked Jenna. It was lying in a heap at the edge of the woods.

"The wind must've blown it down," Jason replied. "I'll go pull out the pegs. You shouldn't, like, exert yourself or anything. Dr. Mom said so."

Jenna smiled. As Jason worked on the tent, she wandered around the clearing, looking for anything they might have dropped in the darkness.

"Jenna?" Jason called. "Jenna, you should—can you come here? Now?"

Jenna crossed the clearing and stood next to Jason as he held up the tent. A terrible gash had nearly ripped it in two. Then something fell to the ground at Jenna's feet. She reached down, slowly, and picked it up.

A razor-sharp talon, speckled with dried blood. *More syrup?* Jenna thought bitterly. *More food coloring? And just when I thought Jason had changed—*

"Jason," she breathed. "Why? Why would you do this?"

"Do what?"

"Hide the talon in the torn tent. Try to scare me."

Jason shook his head. Then he reached into his back pocket and pulled out another talon.

148

The one that Jenna had found in the woods, two weeks ago.

The talon that had started all this.

A sick, sinking sense of dread washed over Jenna; her eyes met Jason's, and a look of unbearable understanding passed between them. She forced herself to take a closer look at the two talons. They were identical, except that the one she had just found was splattered with . . . was it her blood? Or the Marked Monster's?

As if Jenna and Jason could read each other's thoughts, they dropped the talons in the dirt and started to run from the clearing as fast as they could.

It didn't matter, though.

They could never outrun the scratching, coming from deep within the woods, where some . . . thing . . . waited.

It was patient.

It would wait as long as it took.

DO NOT FEAR—

WE HAVE ANOTHER CREEPY TALE FOR YOU!
CONTINUE READING FOR A SNEAK PEEK AT

You're invited to a

CREEPOVER™

Best Friends Forever

It was very early on Saturday morning, and while most other kids were sleeping, Whitney Van Lowe was wide awake, and very busy.

She was unpacking her dolls, which were each in individual plastic boxes inside a larger cardboard box. Each time she opened one, it was like a reunion with an old friend. She felt a special responsibility to make the dolls comfortable in her new home.

"Penelope! I know you don't like being in your box for so long. But see, here you are in the fresh air again. Look, here's your new spot. Right next to your good friend Irene," Whitney spoke soothingly to a doll wearing a sailor suit. "You're all so lucky you don't have to go to school. I know you must hate moving around, but imagine what it's like being me. I'm always the new girl, and I have to work so hard to make new friends."

Whitney looked at one doll in a Mexican embroidered dress. "What, Rosa?" she asked. "Yes, well, it's not as easy as it looks." She paused as if the doll was responding, and then she replied. "Gracias. I think you're a really good friend too!" She sighed. "I'll be back, everyone. I've got to go downstairs for breakfast."

She paused at the door, looking down at all her dolls lined up on the floor. "The name of our new town is Westbrook, everyone, remember?" she spoke like a teacher addressing a class. "It's in Connecticut. The town of Westbrook is on the beach. The body of water is Long Island Sound, and our new house is in the woods. This region of the United States is called New England. Why do you think it's called New England?" She paused.

"That's right, because English settlers moved here and started colonies." She smiled lovingly at her dolls. "Okay, there's obviously something more important that I haven't said." She sounded serious.

"I know I had to pack you in your boxes really fast. It must have been very shocking and scary. And I do know I wasn't very gentle. I'm very sorry about that. But you know that's not the way I would have done it if it had been up to me."

She took a deep breath, and her face clouded over. "I think you know that it was up to my dad, and I think you also know that he can't be trusted."

Then she went downstairs, which looked like Box City. There were towers of boxes everywhere. Her dad had set up his laptop on the kitchen table and was reading something, his brow furrowed. Whitney saw him, but he didn't see her. A strange look flickered across her face as she glimpsed what was on the computer screen.

"Are you reading about Wisconsin again?" Whitney asked.

Her dad quickly closed the laptop cover. He tried to smile, but his worried expression remained. Whitney nodded knowingly. "I know you're concerned about what happened in Wisconsin," she said. "But don't worry. All that's in the past now. All I'm ever going to say about that state is that they make great cheese. And speaking of cheese, what's for breakfast?"

WANT MORE CREEPINESS?

Then you're in luck because P. J. Night has some more scares for you and your friends!

What does the Marked Monster look like? Why don't you and your friends draw it together? Have one friend start by drawing the monster's head, then have another friend draw its body, another its wings, and so on.

YOU'RE INVITED TO . . .
CREATE YOUR OWN SCARY STORY!

Do you want to turn your sleepover into a creepover? Telling a spooky story is a great way to set the mood. P. J. Night has written a few sentences to get you started. Fill in the rest of the story and have fun scaring your friends.

You can also collaborate with your friends on this story by taking turns. Have everyone at your sleepover sit in a circle. Pick one person to start. She will add a sentence or two to the story, cover what she wrote with a piece of paper leaving only the last word or phrase visible, and then pass the story to the next girl. Once everyone has taken a turn, read the scary story you created together aloud!

I remember it like it was yesterday. One minute I was walking through the bright, cheery woods on a lovely spring day. The next, storm clouds had gathered overhead and I could hear rumbling. But it wasn't the rumbling of thunder. It was the sound

of something running behind me, pounding the
earth below it. Something big. I began to run as
fast as I could, but I could feel it gaining on me. I
turned around and saw it. It was . . .

_____

_____

_____

_____

_____

_____

_____

_____

_____

_____

_____

_____

_____

_____

THE END

A lifelong night owl, **P. J. NIGHT** often works furiously into the wee hours of the morning, writing down spooky tales and dreaming up new stories of the supernatural and otherworldly. Although P. J.'s whereabouts are unknown at this time, we suspect the author lives in a drafty, old mansion where the floorboards creak when no one is there and the flickering candlelight creates shadows that creep along the walls. We truly wish we could tell you more, but we've been sworn to keep P. J.'s identity a secret . . . and it's a secret we will take to our graves!

What's better than reading a really spooky story?

Writing your own!

You just read a great book. It gave you ideas, didn't it? Ideas for your next story: characters...plot...setting... You can't wait to grab a notebook and a pen and start writing it all down.

It happens a lot. *Ideas just pop into your head.* In between classes entire story lines take shape in your imagination. And when you start writing, the words flow, and you end up with notebooks crammed with your creativity.

It's okay, you aren't alone. Come to **KidPub**, the web's largest gathering of kids just like you. Share your stories with thousands of people from all over the world. Meet new friends and see what they're writing. Test your skills in one of our writing contests. See what other kids think about your stories.

And above all, *come to write!*

www.KidPub.com